Giants Village

Giants Dam

Kobold Mines

Snake of Wisdom

Brave Hunter
and the Giants

By the same author:

Brave Hunter and the Witches
Brave Hunter and the Dragons
Brave Hunter and the Sea Snakes
Brave Hunter and the Pirates

For more information please visit our website on:

www.Brave-Hunter.co.uk

www.Brave-Hunter.com

Brave Hunter and the Giants

José Hofstede

Illustrations by
Ton Derks

First print 2006

ISBN-10: 90-78346-02-7

ISBN-13: 978-90-78346-02-9

Contents

Brave Hunter lives in the village of Oak-trunk. He is a friendly relaxed man who is always willing to help people. He got his name from being so courageous and fearless. Brave Hunter isn't just extremely strong, but also tremendously smart! One day he got a letter from his uncle from Corsica who asked for his help to chase the pirates from the island. Off course he left straight away to help his relatives. But the journey to Corsica is full of adventures!

Neston is the fourteen-year-old son of the village blacksmith. He is a cheerful lad with brown curly hair and brown twinkley eyes who is always looking for adventure. He follows Brave Hunter to Corsica to fight with the pirates. In Jingleland he learns how to fly with a magic flying stick.

Alice is the fairy princess of Jingleland. She asks Brave Hunter to help them to rid Jingleland from the evil witches. After a happy ending, her parents allow her to travel with Brave Hunter and the others to Wizard County to visit Norma's father.

Norma is a witch girl. Her mother is the good witch Desirée and her father the Mighty Sorcerer of the High Mountain. She has a medallion from her father that protects her against evil. Because Brave Hunter will travel through Wizard County she has the chance to meet her father for the first time.

WHERE HAS ALICE GONE?

The sun, which stood high in the sky, smiled at the high green mountains below her. The mountains were just like enormous giants trying to reach the deep blue sky. The sun radiated her beams onto their peaks, gliding them down across the mountainsides, among the caverns and rocks, over patches of green grass and bushes, to finally reach a mountain track.

As the sun moved to the west, she could see a group of travellers walking along on the mountain-path, with two fully packed horses. One of the horses, which was led by a large man, had a tiny fairy on its back. Behind him walked a young boy with brown curly hair, who was leading the other horse. In front of the man, a young girl with long black hair flew on a broom. The sun focused her beams on the little fairy as she sat on the horse.

"The sun is really bright!", smiled the fairy, who's name was Alice, while she held her hands in front of her eyes. Brave Hunter (*that was the man's name*) nodded cheerfully:

"Indeed, the sun has all ready climbed quite high." He turned around to glance at the boy behind him (*Neston was his name*) who was just patting the horse on its neck.

"Good horsey", he whispered. Brave Hunter smiled and said:

"We will have a short break, at the first open and flat space." Neston looked up and said pleased:

"Great idea, because I am starving!" Norma, the girl with the long black hair, clapped her hands in excitement.

"I will fly ahead to see if there is some flat grassland." She grabbed her broom tightly with both hands and pushed it up. Poof, off she went, up into the sky. Alice chuckled:

"Wow, she must be very hungry, indeed." Brave Hunter clacked his tongue and said cheerfully:

"We have walked a long way after all and that makes one hungry." Alice laughed and responded:

"I am glad that I am little, so I may ride on the horse." Then she looked inquisitively at Brave Hunter.

"How far do we have to travel, Brave Hunter?" Brave Hunter raised his eyebrows and asked:

"You mean to Corsica?" Alice shook her head.

"No, no, how long is it to travel to Norma's father, the Mighty Sorcerer of the High Mountain."

For a brief moment Brave Hunter looked puzzled, but then nodded:

"Of course, that's what you mean!"

Brave Hunter's thoughts wandered to his uncle and aunt in Corsica. A FEW DAYS AGO WHILE HE WAS SITTING IN FRONT OF HIS CABIN IN OAK-TRUNK, HE HAD RECEIVED A LETTER FROM HIS UNCLE ANTONIO. ANTONIO HAD ASKED FOR HIS HELP TO RID THEIR ISLAND OF MEAN PIRATES. IMMEDIATELY BRAVE HUNTER HAD STARTED OUT ON THE ROAD. TO HIS BIG SURPRISE HE DISCOVERED THAT NESTON HAD BEEN FOLLOWING HIM.

NESTON WAS THE SON OF THE BLACKSMITH IN THE VILLAGE OF OAK-TRUNK AND ALWAYS LOOKING FOR ADVENTURE. HE JUST WANTED TO SEND NESTON BACK TO OAK-TRUNK WHEN THEY MET ALICE. ALICE WAS THE DAUGHTER OF THE FAIRY KING AND QUEEN OF JINGLELAND AND HAD BEEN SENT TO ASK FOR HIS HELP. YOU SEE, JINGLELAND WAS BEING PESTERED BY AN EVIL WITCH, WHO CAPTURED LITTLE FAIRIES AND PUT THEM IN GLASS JARS.

WITH THE HELP OF NORMA THEY HAD BEEN ABLE TO FREE JINGLELAND FROM THIS MEAN WITCH. NORMA WAS THE DAUGHTER OF THE GOOD WITCH DESIRÉE AND THE MIGHTY SORCERER OF THE HIGH MOUNTAIN. DESIRÉE HAD GIVEN BRAVE HUNTER A PASS SO HE COULD TRAVEL THROUGH WIZARD COUNTY. THIS WAY THEY COULD CUT OFF A HUGE PIECE OF THE ROAD AND

REACH CORSICA MUCH MORE QUICKLY. NORMA HAD
PLEADED WITH BRAVE HUNTER TO ALLOW HER TO
TRAVEL WITH THEM, TO WIZARD COUNTY, TO SEE HER
FATHER. YOU SEE, SHE NEVER HAD MET HER FATHER
BEFORE AND WAS DESPERATE TO SEE HIM, MORE THEN
ANYTHING ELSE IN WHOLE WIDE WORLD. OF COURSE
BRAVE HUNTER DIDN'T MIND NORMA TRAVELLING
ALONG WITH THEM AND THEN ALICE WANTED TO COME
ALONG AS WELL. THAT IS HOW ALL FOUR OF THEM
WERE NOW TRAVELLING TOGETHER ON THIS NARROW
MOUNTAIN PATH TOWARDS WIZARD COUNTY.

Brave Hunter stared pensively at the view to
his right and answered Alice:

"I think it is about five days travelling." Alice
squinted as she gazed into the distance.

"It looks as if we still have to cross many
mountain passes", she said looking at the
numerous high mountaintops. Brave Hunter
nodded.

"Yep, it will be quite a trip." Then he turned
to Alice and smiled.

"That is why it is so pleasant to have you and
Norma along for company." Alice clapped her
hands in excitement.

"I wouldn't have wanted to miss this trip for
the world." Her cheeks were flushed and her
eyes were twinkling like stars. "I think it is
such a great adventure!"

Just at that moment Norma flew towards

them. She waved enthusiastically with her hand in the air. Brave Hunter waved back and called out:

"And have you seen a nice spot?" Norma nodded and landed her broom in front of Brave Hunter. Her hair was blown in every direction. She got off her broom and wanted to walk next to Brave Hunter. But the path was too narrow for a horse and two people, so she climbed back on her broom and flew low next to him.

"What did you see behind this mountain top?", asked Brave Hunter. Norma flipped her long black hair backwards and answered:

"The next mountain is a bit lower and is flat on the top." She hesitated a bit. "It is a bit odd; it is not really a mountain but more like a crater."

"A crater?", asked Brave Hunter in surprise. "But this isn't a volcanic area!" Norma shook her head while shrugging her shoulders.

"Indeed that is what struck me as peculiar too." She put her forefinger in the air and continued smiling: "But the place has a beautiful patch of grassland where we can have our lunch." Brave Hunter pursed his lips and nodded contently:

"That is just what we are looking for."

After a 30 minute walk, they reached the summit of the mountain and looked at the crater in front of them. The mountain crater looked indeed very different then the other mountains. Surrounded by high, barren rock-like giant mountains, this mountain crater looked like a lovely infant hill. Covered with rolling meadows and many varieties of trees and bushes. There were two small mountain lakes. The blue sky reflected in the water.

After walking a little bit further the group stood in front of one of the lakes. Neston got the packing, the saddle and the bridle off the horses. The horses trotted straight to the lake and feasted themselves on the cool, fresh mountain water and then helped themselves to the abundant juicy grass. Alice and Norma unpacked the baskets. They spread a large blue cloth on the ground in the sunlight. Four cups and four bowls decorated the cloth. They laid out two jars, one filled with soup and the other with tea. On a large plate they placed various fillings for sandwiches and an apple and a peach for each person.

Brave Hunter sat on the large picnic cloth with his back against a rock. He took the map, which he was given by the fairy king, out of his rucksack and unfolded it on the cloth. Neston sat beside him and poured the soup into the four bowls. Norma took the other jar and poured tea into the cups, while Alice flew above the map to study it carefully.

"Here we are", explained Brave Hunter, while he pointed his finger at a spot on the map, "and we should arrive here tonight." His finger was sliding over the map. "There is the log cabin, where we are going to stay the night." Alice called out in excitement:

"I always find log cabins so cosy!" Her wings were fluttering up and down in excitement setting off the sound of tiny bells as they whisked through the air. Then she dropped to the cloth and grabbed a sandwich from the dish.

Neston was staring at the map, his head bent.

"Hmmm, how much further is it walking, Brave Hunter?", he asked. Brave Hunter took a slurp of his soup.

"I guess two or three hours." He reached out, grabbed a sandwich and continued: "We will be there by the end of the day for sure." Then he took a large bite of the sandwich and mumbled contently: "Alice's mother can sure make delicious sandwiches." Alice laughed nodding in agreement while taking a piece of apple and flew into the direction of the horses.

After a short rest Brave Hunter jumped up.

"Come on, let's get moving, I want to be at the log cabin before dark." Norma packed up the baskets and Neston and Brave Hunter saddled the horses and tied the packs. When they had finished Brave Hunter looked around a little concerned and asked:

"Does anybody know where Alice has flown to?" Norma, who had just strapped the baskets onto the horses, turned around.

"I saw her flying to the horses, but after that I didn't pay any attention." Neston shook his head.

"I didn't see her fly away at all", he answered in surprise.

Brave Hunter cupped his hands around his mouth and shouted out loud:

"Alice, where are you? We are leaving now!" No answer. Again he yelled: "Alice, come on, we really have to go now!" All three were silent as mice, listening to a sign of life from Alice. But they didn't hear anything at all. There was only silence. Neston looked around puzzled and asked:

"Where is she?"

Brave Hunter had a worried look on his face and nodded to Norma.

"Please could you fly over the crater and look around?"

"Of course!", answered Norma spontaneously and jumped on her broom. She first flew around the crater. Then she flew straight over it and disappeared behind the mountain. Then from the back up again and flew over the mountain. Eventually she landed in front of Brave Hunter and Neston. She got off her broom and shook her long hair.

"I don't see any sign of Alice", she said with a sad voice. "It seems as if she has disappeared completely." Neston looked attentively at Norma and finally asked:

"Can't you use your magic to bring her back here?" Norma shook her head and said decidedly:

"No, I don't have that power." Neston frowned and kicked a small stone while he mumbled:

"I wish we had a dog that could track down Alice." Norma looked at Neston with wide eyes and suddenly jumped up.

"Oh, but that I can do!", she yelled in excitement. Neston looked at her in surprise.

"You can work your magic and get us a dog?" Norma shook her head:

"No, I can't wizard a dog like that. But I can change a mouse or something else into a dog!" Brave Hunter called out to one of the horses that trotted towards them.

"Can you change this horse into a dog?" Norma pursed her lips and nodded slowly:

"That should work." She put herself in front of the horse, waved her arms in the air and said in a clear voice:

"Horse brown and heavy as a log,
from now on you will be a tracker dog."

In a flash a misty cloud appeared around the horse and when the cloud had dissolved, a brown dog wagging his tail, stood in front of them. Norma clapped her hands in joy:

"It worked!" The dog barked excitedly at Norma.

In the meantime Neston had walked to the baskets and got one of Alice's dresses. He walked back to the dog and pushed the dress under its nose.

"Search doggy, search, find Alice." The dog started enthusiastically sniffing at the dress. When he had sniffed enough he started to bark and pulled his head backwards.

"He wants us to follow him", Brave Hunter said to the others, while he took a step in the direction of the dog. The dog barked again, turned around and started to run, while his nose sniffed the ground and air. The three friends ran after him until the dog stopped near the crater and barked impatiently, while he jumped up and down.

They could see a big hole where the dog was standing.

"Do you think that Alice has fallen into that hole?", Neston asked while panting out of breath. Norma shrugged her shoulders in surprise:

"But she can fly!" Brave Hunter went down

on his knees in front of the hole.

"It is not a rabbit hole", he determined immediately while gazing into the hole.

"But I can't imagine that Alice would have fallen into it", he said decisively to the others. Then he looked into the hole again and shouted loudly:

"Alice, are you there?" The sound seemed to carry far. "It sounds as if this hole is leading somewhere, as if this is a corridor", Brave Hunter said while he got up again. He looked at Neston and Norma with a disturbed face. "It looks as if she has been dragged by something or someone into this corridor."

ALICE MEETS LAUREN.

After Alice had given each horse a piece of apple, she flew towards the crater. She saw a couple of White Mountain flowers and flew towards them.

"Hmm, they really smell sweet", she said softly to herself.

"You also smell nice", squeaked a voice behind her suddenly. With a jerk Alice turned around and saw a little fellow standing behind her. The little guy was about four times bigger then Alice but surely seven times smaller then Neston. He was wearing green knickerbockers and a yellow blouse with laces. Over the blouse he wore a red jacket and on his head he had a green beret. He was carrying a blue rucksack. The rucksack was almost the same colour as his skin.

"Who are you?", Alice asked in surprise.

"My name is Lauren, I am a kobold." He gave a deep bow. Alice blinked.

"A kobold? Do you live under the ground?" Lauren smiled, while he pointed towards a hole in the ground.

"Yes, that is the entrance." Then he took Alice by the hand and pulled her towards the entrance.

"Come on, I will show you our world under

the ground." Alice struggled:

"I can't do that; my friends are waiting for me." But Lauren didn't want to hear about it and said resolutely:

"I like you, I will take you with me." He grabbed Alice and put her in his rucksack. Then he put his rucksack back on and started to walk fast.

In the beginning it was really dark in the rucksack. But slowly it became lighter. After a while Alice heard other voices in the distance.

"Ah, there you are, we were looking all over for you." It was a woman's voice. Alice heard Lauren responding:

"I was just playing, mum." The woman took Lauren by the arm and pushed him forwards.

"Hop to it, go change yourself Lauren. The ceremony starts in 10 minutes."

Lauren started to walk fast. Alice bounced back and forwards in the rucksack. Then Lauren stood still and she heard a door opening, a climbing of steps and then another door opening again. Lauren took of his rucksack and put it down.

"You can come out now! Welcome to my little hideaway", he said cheerfully, while he took Alice out of the rucksack. Carefully he put Alice on his bed. She was a little bit shaken up by it all and rubbed her eyes.

When her eyes were a bit more used to the light she looked around her and saw that she was standing on a little bed. The bed was covered with a crochet bedspread. She saw at the left of the room a wooden desk with a book-case filled with books next to it. In the middle of the room was a small low table with coloured candles on it and cushions around it.

This was obviously the place where Lauren entertained his friends.

The room and the ceiling were round. It seemed as if the room was cut out of mountain rock and that they were sitting in a sort of cave. There were no windows at all in the room. The room was lit by glow-worms who were stuck to the wall and ceiling.

When Alice had recovered from the shock, she looked angrily at Lauren.

"Why did you take me? We, my friends and I, are on our way to the Mighty Sorcerer of the High Mountain." She pointed her forefinger into the air. "And we are in a terrible hurry! Because Brave Hunter has to rid the pirates from the island of Corsica." Alice sat on the bed and put her head in her hands and said sadly:

"My friends must be worried sick by now, wondering where I am." Lauren looked sorrow-fully at Alice and dropped his shoulders. Then he said softly:

"I thought that you were so cute and sweet,

that I wanted to take you with me." Alice shook her head and responded angrily:

"You just can't take someone with you when you feel like it!" Then she started to cry softly. Quickly Lauren took out a handkerchief and handed it over to Alice.

"I do have to go now to the ceremony, but as soon as that is finished I will take you back", he stammered.

"How long will that be?", she asked in a high-pitched voice. Lauren raised his shoulders and shook his head.

"That depends. It differs every time."

Then he turned around and walked to the door.

"I really have to go now, otherwise I will be too late." He opened the door and turned around one more time.

"Please, don't leave this room, because that can be very dangerous!" Alice nodded slowly and mumbled:

"I will see what I will do."

THE KOBOLD'S CEREMONY

Once Lauren was out of the door Alice flew from the bed.

"If you think that I'll stay here waiting for your return, Lauren, then you are very wrong!", she said softly to herself. She flew to the door and turned the handle. Carefully she opened the door and looked into a corridor, which had three doors. Like the room, the corridor was cut out of mountain rock. The ceiling was decorated with figures. And on the wall and ceiling were glow-worms that lit up the hall. It was dead quiet in the cave-house.

Alice flew to one of the doors and opened it softly. This room also had the shape of a cave. There was a large bed in the middle of the room. On one side of the room was a large closet and on the other side stood a dressing table with all kinds of perfume and make-up bottles on top.

"This must be the bedroom of Lauren's mother and father", Alice thought as she closed the door again. In excitement Alice flew to the other door and opened it carefully. It turned out to be a girl's room.

"Hmm, Lauren has a sister." Behind the last door was the bathroom. It was the weirdest bathroom Alice ever had seen. The whole bathroom was actually one big bath-tub. Along the smooth round wall, water was dripping down. In the bath-tub was an opening with a plug next to it. The round ceiling was covered with green round emeralds. Also the tub itself had green emeralds. Only those emeralds were flat so you could sit on them. Blue moss was growing on the wall. The glow-worms were shining on the emeralds and that made the whole bathroom glow with green light. On a shelf stood two ceramic oil holders which spread a delightful scent through the room.

Alice closed the door behind her and flew down the corridor to the stairs and then flew down the stairs. She came into some sort of hall with had a big front door. Cautiously Alice opened the front door and gazed outside. She saw a narrow street, cut out of the mountain rock. There were windows and doors in the walls.

"Looks as if those are the houses of the other kobolds", thought Alice. The street was lit by glow-worms, who were nestled into the curved ceiling. Their light reflected against the precious stones, which were scattered all over the ceiling. It gave the street a magical glow.

Alice peered down the street and looked from left to right. She could see no-one and there was not a sound to be heard.

"Not a single soul around", Alice thought in relief. "Lauren was talking about a ceremony. This is my chance to fly back to the world above the ground." Alice flew further into the street, which lead to a square. In the middle of the square stood a large statue of a kobold, decorated with all kinds of precious stones. Around the square were shops, cafés and restaurants, all cut out of the mountain rock. In front of the cafés and restaurants were chairs and tables. Nobody sat on a chair, not a single kobold in sight. It was all deserted. There were four streets leading out of the square.

"Which one will take me to the exit where I came from?", Alice pondered. One of the streets went up quite steeply. She decided to take that one. After a couple of minutes flying, the street suddenly bent downwards.

"This can't be the right way", Alice decided and just wanted to turn around when she heard some noise.

"The kobolds must be there!", Alice whispered to herself in surprise.

It would have been wise of Alice to turn around now and follow another street. But curiosity got the better of her and she flew closer and closer to the sound.

"Just for a minute", she mused, "just to see what that secret ceremony is all about."

She flew further and further down the steep road. It felt as if it was leading to the centre of the earth. Eventually she arrived into a large room, which looked like a ballroom. From the ceiling limestone stalactites, in all kinds of bizarre shades, were dripping. The floor was slippery from the dripping water. There were also huge stalagmites standing on the ground, formed by the dripping limewater of the ceiling. It was cold and the air smelled a little stale. Suddenly she heard the sound of a roaring crowd.

Alice quickly crossed the ballroom and came to a very large corridor. She flew into the corridor and at the end she saw a large crowd of kobolds gathered around a huge underground lake. Quickly Alice hid behind one of the lime stalagmites. With large eyes and mouth open wide she looked at the spectacle. An underground stream trickled into the lake.

The water in the lake was very low. In the middle of the lake was a wooden platform, which was connected to a landing on one side. Above the platform hung two long cords from a hole in the ceiling, on the left of the lake was a waterwheel that scooped up water into pitchers. The pitchers emptied the water into a wooden pipe that ran into the wall. But the water in the lake was so low that the pitchers

were hardly filled.

Alice saw a kobold climbing up the landing. He looked really important. He wore a beautiful green cloak, decorated with golden thread. On his head he had a helmet, which was strewn with diamonds and rubies.

"He must be the king of the country", Alice thought. She saw the kobold raising his hands into the air and starting to speak to the crowd.

"Dear fellow earthmen, look here at the fruit of our hard labour." He picked up the basket, which was filled with all kinds of precious stones. Even in the dim light the stones were shining in the basket. The king continued in a trembling voice:

"Again we send another load of precious stones to the giants. I know you all would rather see it differently but we just don't have any other choice. They control the water and without water we cannot live."

The king paused for a while and looked into the crowd before him with a grave face. He threw his hands up, with both his fore-fingers sticking out, as if he were conducting a choir.

"I ask you all to sing our national anthem, loud enough that the giants will hear it. And show them that you are proud to be a kobold!"

The king put is right hand on his left shoulder and started to sing at the top of his voice. Everyone joined him and the whole space was filled with the song. You could tell that the kobolds were very moved, because many had to blink away the tears that filled their eyes.

> *"Our country is under the ground,*
> *our homes are nice and round.*
> *All day we work in the mine,*
> *which we think is really fine.*
> *After work we drink kobold rum,*
> *we play and laugh and have lots of fun.*
> *We kobolds are very proud,*
> *so we sing this song out loud."*

The king picked up the basket and tied it to the cord that was dangling above his head and then pulled on the cord without the basket. The basket was pulled up and disappeared into the hole in the ceiling. The crowd was deathly quiet. It took some minutes but then suddenly the river started to flow strongly and the lake started to fill with clear cool water. The kobolds clapped their hands and cheered:

"Yippee, we have water again!"

Alice who was sitting very quietly behind the stalagmites, thought in surprise:

"Giants?"

THE GROUP IS TAKEN PRISONER.

Brave Hunter stood with a little case of mother-of-pearls in his hand. He took some magic powder out of the case, put it in the palm of his hand and blew the powder onto Neston's hair. Immediately Neston started to shrink. Brave Hunter got the magic powder from the fairy king of Jingleland. Then he sprinkled himself with the magic powder. Neston and Brave Hunter were now small enough to go through the hole.

"What are you waiting for?", Neston asked Norma impatiently. She nodded quickly and made a gesture with her hands and mumbled some words. For a while she was veiled in mist and when the mist had cleared Norma was small enough to go through the hole.

"Can you work your magic and get us some lanterns?", Brave Hunter asked. Norma waved her hands again and before you could blink your eyes, three lanterns were standing on the grass. Everyone took one lantern.

"Shall we go then?", Neston proposed, while he walked into the hole. Brave Hunter and Norma were following him. "It is indeed a very dark corridor", Neston mumbled, while he shone his lantern back and forward. "There is

nothing to see but rock, rock and more rock."
Brave Hunter pushed him in the back.

"Come on Neston move on, we have to find
Alice as soon as possible." Carefully they
continued into the corridor. After only a couple
of steps the corridor got wider and lighter.

"Hey, glow-worms", said Neston pleased as
he shone his lantern on the ceiling.

"Look it is lighter a little further down!",
called Norma enthusiastically, as she pointed
forward. Brave Hunter waved his lantern
around and growled contently:

"Let's go quickly." They arrived at the same
square where Alice just had been.

"Wow, a whole village under the ground!",
shouted Neston full of surprise and
admiration.

They looked around themselves in amazement.

"Pubs, restaurants, shops", Norma listed
while she took in the surrounding.

"And they are all cut out of the rocks",
Neston observed.

"Hmm", Brave Hunter squinted. "I have
never seen so many precious stones gathered."

He walked to the centre of the square.

"Look here, this statue is covered with
rubies, emeralds, sapphires and diamonds."
Excitedly Neston pointed to the doors and the

windows. The doors and the windows are also covered with precious stones." Brave Hunter nodded in wonder:

Who lives under the ground?" Norma took a step forward, put on a grave face and replied in a clear voice:

"Here under the earth live the kobolds, or earth-gnomes. But......" Norma paused for a bit, looked around in surprise and continued:

"Where are they?" Brave Hunter shrugged his shoulders hesitantly, while rubbing his chin and said cautiously:

"So, an earth-gnome has taken Alice. But why?" Norma shook her head and pulled a puzzled face.

"I have no idea. They are usually friendly and pleasant creatures."

Just at that moment they heard a bunch of noise at the other end of the square. The noise was coming from the kobolds just returning from the underground lake. The king's body-guard saw them first and yelled immediately:

"Intruders, intruders in our kingdom, intruders in our kingdom!" He sprinted forward while he shouted:

"Get them!" A couple of kobolds ran with him.

Before Brave Hunter, Neston and Norma realised what hit them they had handcuffs on.

Then they were dragged into a street and eventually stopped at a big iron door, which was also built into the rock. The king's bodyguard knocked on the iron door.

"Prison keeper, please open the door, I have a couple of guests for you." There was no reaction. One of the other kobolds proposed:

"You have to knock a little bit harder, you know Roland is stone-deaf." Again the bodyguard knocked on the door and yelled out on the top of his lungs.

"Open the door!" Then they heard somebody shuffling on the other side of the door. There was some clicking of a bunch of keys; one was put into the lock. Some crunching in the lock and the big heavy door swung open with a lot of creaking and noise.

An aged kobold stood in the doorway. His grey hair stuck out from under a red beret. He had a little round pair of glasses on his nose. He was leaning on a cane and in the other hand he held a horn. He put the beginning of the horn, which was very small, in his ear. Then he turned the end of the horn, which was wide, towards the bodyguard and yelled:

"What did you say?" The bodyguard cupped his mouth in his hands and yelled into the horn:

"I have some guests for you." He pointed at Brave Hunter, Neston and Norma. The old man

looked attentively at them one by one, waved his cane in the air and rasped:

"Intruders hey, all rubies in the air!" He frowned, turned around and waved them to follow him.

After they had walked through a long corridor they arrived in a big room with three cells. Each was put in a different cell.

"What are you going to do with us?", Brave Hunter asked the bodyguard in a deep voice. The bodyguard looked straight at Brave Hunter and answered coolly:

"Our king will make that judgement." Then he turned around with a jerk and roared at Roland:

"Keep watching them and don't let them escape." Roland brought the horn to his ear and asked in a squeaky voice:

"You would like some cake?" The bodyguard shook his head in irritation.

"No, you must not let them escape!" Roland nodded his head reassuringly:

"No, I won't let them bake a cake." The bodyguard shrugged his shoulders in despair and stalked off.

When everybody had left the room Norma asked the others:

"Shall I work my magic and open the locks?" Neston jumped up enthusiastically:

"Great idea, so we can escape straight away."
But Brave Hunter shook his head and answered quietly:

"No, that is not a good plan." He put his head through the bars as far as he could so the others could see him better.

"Then we still don't have Alice. And we have to find out what has happened to her." He clasped the bars with both fists and asked:

"Norma, kobolds are kind creatures, right?" Norma nodded in agreement:

"Yes, as far as I know." She pursed her lips and looked puzzled. "I do find it very strange that we are greeted in such a hostile way. They are known for their hospitality."

Neston stroked his fingers over the bars. It made a pling, plong noise. Brave Hunter looked at Neston's musical performance and said calmly:

"I think the best thing to do right now is to wait for the king. He might know what happened to Alice."

ALICE IN THE KOBOLD KING'S PALACE

Lauren ran back home as fast as his legs could carry him. He had seen the bodyguard grabbing the intruders.

"They must be Alice's friends", he thought immediately. "Oh, I wish I had not taken Alice with me", he thought contritely. If the king found out that he had taken strangers into their country under the earth, he would get extremely upset. Especially now, the king had enough to worry about with those giants always pestering them. He quickly had to bring Alice back to the earth above and free her three friends as well.

Lauren opened the front door of his home. His parents and his little sister were still not home.

"They are of course chatting away in the square", Lauren pondered while he walked up the stairs. The king will be too busy to listen to the intruders right away because tonight the council of the F.J.E. (*Fairness, Justice and Equality*) were meeting. So, he, Lauren, had to act quickly. First he had to get Alice and then liberate her friends.

"Alice, I am back!", Lauren shouted out loud as he opened the door of his room. Puzzled he looked around.

"Alice, you don't have to hide yourself, it is me", he said with a hint of doubt in his voice. "Alice, come on out, I am getting impatient!" Lauren looked around his room with an irritated face, but no Alice was to be seen. A feeling of panic came over him.

"Oh goodness me, she did leave the room without me! Where can she be now?", he thought nervously.

At that very same moment Alice was sitting stock-still behind the stalagmite. The last kobold had just left the area. After the lake had been filled with water, the king had given another speech. A very important meeting was going to take place tonight. He had promised the kobolds that things were going to change. How and when Alice had not understood.

She looked around her. The area was unpleasantly empty with all the kobolds gone. The water rippled peacefully against the edge of the basin. The basin was now filled with water all the way to the edge. The water wheel with the pitchers was working overtime. Splash, scoop it went and then the pitchers were emptied into the wooden tube.

"The water will go to the kobolds houses", Alice thought. Then she shook her head. "Think Alice, think", she mumbled to herself.

"How do I get back above the ground, to Brave Hunter, Neston and Norma?"

She decided to fly back to the square first. She again crossed the ballroom and went back into the street she had flown through earlier. When she was back at the square she saw that this time it was packed with kobolds. Alice hid in a little dark corner. There were kobolds all around, busy chatting to one and another. Some were sitting at a table, others were leaning on a bar and others were standing in the middle of the square. A few were sitting around the statue.

"What a business", Alice sighed, "I'll never get away unseen!" At that same moment there was the sound of a trumpet blaring:
"Tatrata, tatrata." Within seconds, everybody in the square was deathly quiet. Alice saw a kobold in uniform to her left with a trumpet in his hand. He was standing at attention. He was a herald, a message bringer. He called out:
"Attention, attention! I announce the arrival of the board members off the F.J.E. Council"

He saluted and stepped aside. An elf passed him. He had a long white beard and was wearing a blue overall with a yellow jacket. On his head he wore a red pointed cap with a large bob on the tip.

The herald put his hand to his mouth and said in a loud voice:

"I announce the representative of the elves." Loud applause sounded over the square. Behind the elf walked two animals; an owl and a squirrel. Alice heard the herald shouting in the distance:

"The representatives of the animals of the forest." But her eyes were focussed on the squirrel.

"But, but, that is Pim", Alice whispered in surprise.

She squeezed her eyes together, looked more closely and nodded in excitement.

"Yes without any doubt, that is Pim!" Alice looked pleased at the party that was approaching her.

"Oh, this is wonderful, now Pim is here everything will turn out all right."

Pim, the squirrel, was a close friend of her parents. Once a month he would visit Jingleland and stayed then with them in the palace. Pim always knew the latest news and was very well informed about new events. He was a real storyteller. His stay at the palace was always a big event. At night, when everybody had their supper, they all went to the chamber of knights. Pim sat in the special storyteller armchair and filled the evening with tales about his adventures. Everybody listened in a breathless hush. Every time Pim had visited them Alice dreamed that she was the one who was experiencing all those wonderful adventures. But at the moment she was not dreaming at all. No, this time she was really caught up into an exciting adventure of her own.

The elf was passing her now. She looked further down and tried to get eye contact with Pim. Suddenly he saw her standing and shouted out in amazement:

"Alice, what on earth are you doing here?" Alice didn't think twice, ran towards him and threw her arms around his neck.

"I am so glad to see you here", she sobbed relieved. "A kobold has brought me here against my will. I have to go back above the ground as quickly as possible. I have friends waiting there for me", she rattled on. "And we don't have much time because we have to go to the Mighty Sorcerer of the High Mountain, that is Norma's father. And Brave Hunter and Neston have to free Corsica from the pirates. And I am here now and they don't know where I am."

She looked at Pim with big tear-filled eyes and asked anxiously:

"Oh please, can't you take me back above

the ground? Back to my friends?" Pim stared at her in bewilderment.

"Well, well, well, that is quite a story you tell there, pirates, sorcerers." He nodded his head:

"Don't you worry, we will get you back to your friends above the ground."

The owl, who had followed the whole story, asked curiously:

"Who is this lovely fairy?" Pim waved his tail and responded:

"You know her, she is the daughter of the fairy king." A smile appeared around the beak of the owl.

"Of course, the last time I saw you, you were such a little thing, you didn't even have wings. But my my, you have grown a lot!" Pim took Alice by the hand and said cheerfully:

"Alice, you come along with us and after the meeting I will take you back above the ground myself." Alice dried her tears and happily gambolled along with Pim.

The same kobold that had been standing on the scaffold walked towards them.

"Good day your majesty", the elf greeted the king, while putting out his hand. "It is a great honour meeting you again." The king shook the elf's hand and tapped him kindly on the shoulders.

"I see that you have brought somebody with

you", he said amused to Pim while he pointed at Alice. Pim shook his head:

"No majesty, I didn't bring her along but I have met her here. One of your kobolds has taken her with him, against her will." He pushed Alice, who had been hiding behind his fluffy tail, forward.

"This is Alice, the daughter of the king of Jingleland."

The kobold king scratched his cheek.

"Hmm, maybe those three intruders are your friends." Alice's face lit up and she asked inquisitively:

"Three intruders? Are they Brave Hunter, Neston and Norma? A human, a child human and a child witch?" The king shrugged his shoulders and shook his head.

"I have no idea, I only saw them in the distance." Then he turned around to one of his bodyguards and asked:

"Those intruders were they a man, a boy and a girl?" The bodyguard nodded:

"That is correct your majesty." The king frowned and said decisively:

"Please fetch them for me!" The bodyguard raised his eyebrows in surprise.

"Right now?" The king nodded and answered brusquely:

"Yes, right now!" He turned again to Alice and said with a smile:

"We will soon know if they are your friends."
He walked forward, put his hand in the air and
said with dignity:

"Dear friends, please follow me."

After a little stroll they came to a large gate
in the wall. The gate opened and they stepped
into a hallway with many, many doors. A footman opened one of the doors that lead to a long
corridor with a very low ceiling. There were
many diamonds in the ceiling, which were lit
by the glow-worms, so the corridor was clearly
lit.

After a little while the long corridor curved
slightly downwards and eventually they arrived
in a big round room. Here too the ceiling was
covered with diamonds. A large diamond
chandelier hung in the middle of the room. In
the wall, which was covered with rubies and
emeralds, various torches were sticking out.
There was a big bar in the corner; behind the
bar was a kobold cleaning glasses. In the back
of the room was a large fireplace with logs
burning in it. Around the fireplace were seven
green armchairs with fluffy, comfy pillows.
Next to each arm-chair, was a small marble
table with a dish on it. The dishes were filled
with nuts, raisins and carrots. The king
flopped on the fluffy pillow of one of the armchairs and waved to his guests.

"Please gentlemen, sit down!" Then he signalled to the barman and asked the others:

"What would you like to drink?" Within an eye-blink the barman was standing next to the king.

"For me one of those Bubbly Azules Shakes", the king said merrily to him. The barman nodded and then looked at the elf, who pursed his lips and looked inquisitively at the king.

"Bubbly Azules Shake?" The king slapped both his hands on his upper leg and started to explain with great enthusiasm.

"Yes it is the most delicious drink you will ever taste." He licked his lips. "Hmm, it is a mixture of carrot juice, rose hip extract and kobold-beer." The elf nodded approvingly and said:

"I would like to taste that delicious Bubbly Azules Shake." Also the owl and Pim took the national cocktail and Alice got a glass of lemonade.

When everybody was sipping on their drink the king asked:

"Did you have a good journey?" The elf, who just had taken a big sip, growled:

"Hmm, this is very good stuff." And again he took a deep gulp. The owl, who had not yet tasted the cocktail, took the floor.

"Yes your majesty, we have had a very good journey, Pim and I." The owl nodded towards

Pim. "We met the elf at the crossroad." The owl took on a distinguished look and continued: "Off course we have been talking at length about the giants." The king waved impatiently and shrugged.

"I don't want to talk about that now." He raised his cocktail glass and shouted cheerfully to the barman: "Please, fill it up and also fill up the glasses of my friends here. He pointed with his forfinger to the glasses of the others. The   barman filled all the glasses right to the top. Pim sipped his drink and thought in amusement:

"The king is really living up to his nickname, king Party-Feast."

The owl looked in irritation at the king and the elf, who were both raising their glasses and shouting out exuberant 'CHEERS'. He had, after all, come here to discuss serious matters and not fill himself up with all sorts of drinks. He threw a sideways glance at Pim, who gave him a wink. The owl scratched his throat and started to speak again.

"It is indeed a very difficult situation, we find ourselves in." The elf, whose nose was already turning a little red, hiccupped:

"Yes, do I drink it in one gulp or two?" The kobold king laughed loudly, holding his belly and shaking, while their glasses were filled again.

LAUREN WANTS TO FREE
THE THREESOME.

In the meantime Lauren had walked towards the prison. He wanted to free Brave Hunter, Neston and Norma and hammered his fists on the big gate.

"Roland, open up!" At that same moment Roland sat in the kitchen making a sandwich. He had just spread on it a big layer of peanut butter and on top of that a lot of jam.

"Hmm, delicious", he mumbled, while he poured some milk into a cup. "Oh, a kobold sure gets hungry after all that commotion." He cut the sandwich into little pieces and was just about to take a big bite when he heard knocking on the door.

"Yeah, yeah, yeah", grumbled Roland, while he grabbed his cane, "what the heck do they want from me now?"

When he opened the gate door he saw Lauren, who was very excited, hopping from one leg to the other.

"I am here to get the three prisoners", Lauren said impatiently. Roland shook his head and put the horn in his ear. Lauren bent forward and yelled into the horn:

"I have come to get the three prisoners." Roland nodded and said absentmindedly:

"All right, come along."

"Could you please leave me alone with them for a little while?", asked Lauren when they were in the prison-room. Roland didn't have to think twice and shuffled straight back to the kitchen to finish eating one of those delicious sandwiches.

"And who are you?", roared Brave Hunter when Roland was gone. "The representative of the king?" Lauren shook his head.

"No, no I have come to free you from this prison, so you can go back to where you came from." Neston looked at Lauren in surprise and asked in disbelief:

"Is the king letting us go now?" Lauren looked guilty, bent his head and said softly:

"The king doesn't know anything about it."

"But why do you want to free us then?" Norma wanted to know. Lauren picked nervously at his jacket and straightened his beret.

"Because it is my fault that you have been taken prisoner", he said ashamedly. Brave Hunter frowned and asked sternly:

"Are you the one who has kidnapped Alice?" Lauren nodded while he looked uncomfortably at the floor. Neston grabbed the bars and looked at Lauren tensely:

"Where is she now?" Hesitantly Lauren shrugged his shoulders and stuttered:

"I had left her in my room, but she is not

there anymore." Brave Hunter started to turn red in anger and roared at Lauren:

"What! How could you take her with you and then leave her alone?" Lauren took a step back in fright.

"Eh, eh, I just wanted to play with her", he stuttered. And then with more force in his voice he continued: "I think she went back up." He looked around and grinned shyly:

"So if I free you now you can go up straight away and meet her there." He sighed deeply. "Then the king won't find out that I took strangers into our country." Brave Hunter looked sternly at Lauren and growled on:

"And if Alice did not go up, but is still wandering around here somewhere?"

Brave Hunter just finished the last word when there was a hard knock on the door.

"Open up in the name of the king!"

"Are they already coming to get you?", Lauren said in surprise and fright. He looked around him nervously.

"I have to hide myself, because if they find me I will be in big trouble." Neston clacked his tongue and looked around.

"I don't see where you can hide here." Then he looked at Norma and asked:

"Can't you make him invisible or something?" Norma shook her head:

"No, I cannot make him invisible, but I can

turn him in to something else." Neston gestured with his hands.

"Quick, turn him into a mouse." He pointed at the rucksack Brave Hunter was carrying. "He can hide in there." They heard Roland opening the door.

"Hurry", Lauren panted in panic, "they will be here any moment." Norma put her hands in the air and spoke a magic spell. When the misty cloud had lifted there stood a little mouse with a small beret on. Swiftly Brave Hunter took off his rucksack and laid it open on the ground. The mouse hopped straight in.

Brave Hunter had just put his rucksack on when the door opened and the king's bodyguard stepped in.

"You all have to come with me!", he said grumpily. In the meantime Roland walked further into the room and looked around in a daze.

"Where did Lauren go?", he mumbled to himself in wonder. "I thought I had let him in?" Investigating, Roland shuffled around the room. The bodyguard had no idea what Roland was talking about and reacted in irritation:

"What are you mumbling? There is nobody else here but the prisoners." Roland shook his head not understanding it at all, then sighed deeply and shuffled back to the kitchen and his sandwich.

A NEW PLAN IS HATCHED.

In the palace the crowd was merry. The elf was telling a funny story with all kinds of gory details. Even the owl had to laugh. The king rubbed away a tear and snorted with laughter.

"You can certainly tell a tale my friend." For a little while it became quiet in the room. Then the king clapped his hands together and pulled a serious face. He looked at the visitors one by one and said:

"But the reason why we are here together is very serious indeed." The party nodded in agreement. "Let's first summarise the situation and then we will make a plan of action. Does everyone agree?" The king looked around the circle.

"That seems like a good way to begin", the owl agreed as the others nodded in approval.

At that moment there was a knock on the door. The bodyguard walked in together with Brave Hunter, Neston and Norma. Immediately Alice flew to Brave Hunter and hugged him tightly.

"When the king was speaking about three intruders, I thought that it had to be you." Alice turned around smiling to the king. "They are indeed my friends." The king nodded smiling at Alice and waved at the bodyguard.

"Please take them quickly above the ground." A footman wanted to open the door to let the party go out but Alice flew towards the king.

"Majesty, I have seen your ceremony." The king looked puzzled, but she continued quickly: "and I understand that there are major problems with the giants." She quickly threw a glance at Brave Hunter. "Perhaps Brave Hunter can help you with your   problems? He is very strong and smart and has freed our country of the mean witches."

Brave Hunter took a step forward and shook his head.

"Alice, I really can't fight giants and besides we have to go as quickly as possible to Corsica." Alice flew towards Brave Hunter.

"But you don't have to fight them. Maybe you have a clever idea that the Council can use." Brave Hunter bit his lip.

"I really would like to help the king and give advice." He quickly rubbed his chin. "But I don't know anything about giants." Neston, who had been listening quietly so far, pulled on Brave Hunter's coat:

"But the least we can do is listen to what they have to say." Brave Hunter nodded at Neston.

"Off course, but I don't think that the king is wanting my advice."

"Oh, but I think he is!", squealed the owl. He pointed a wing to an armchair. "Please, take a seat, my dear fellow."

"Yes, we can use any help we can get", the king said enthusiastically. "I really would like to take advantage of your talents."

Brave Hunter looked around the room, nodded and said smiling, while he walked to the armchair:

"In that case I would consider it an honour to help you." The kobold king looked at the owl and asked:

"Would you like to explain what is going on?" The owl looked proudly around and puffed his chest out.

"Well, this is the situation", he started his story. "A couple of years ago the giants built a giant dam on top of the mountain. With this dam they blocked the water flow to the brooks, channels and rivers that run into our countries. From one day to the next we didn't have any water anymore. The giants approached us with a large package of demands.

They demanded the following: The elves had to weave carpets for them; the kobolds had to bring them baskets full of precious stones; and from us, the animals in the forest, they wanted nuts, seeds and fruit. If we fulfilled these demands they would open up the dam, so we would have water again." The owl sipped on his drink, cleared his throat and continued:

"Because we didn't have a choice, we did as we were told. But the giants became greedier and greedier all the time. And now they have come to the point that they close off the dam every other week, until we have delivered all the goods." The elf nodded fiercely and said sadly:

"We just can't bring it up anymore and they refuse to discuss it with us." The king who just nibbled on a nut, joined in:

"And because we have to work all day in the mines, we don't have enough time to look for food." Also the squirrel Pim, who had not said much until now, added:

"Indeed, our own winter supply has as good as disappeared."

Brave Hunter scratched himself behind the ears and had a worried look on his face.

"Gosh, this is indeed quite a problem!" He looked around the group and said seriously: "They are too strong to defeat, so we have to come up with a list." Brave Hunter was thinking deeply, he had a deep frown on his face. It was dead quiet in the room you could hear a needle drop. Then at once he snapped his fingers and asked the king:

"Do you have a map of the surroundings of

the dam?" The king nodded and answered:

"Sure, we do." He turned to the footman and asked:

"Can you bring us a map of the giant village and of the dam?" The footman left the room and came back a few minutes later with a bunch of rolls under his arm. Brave Hunter unrolled them and with Neston standing next to him, studied the maps for a while.

Finally Brave Hunter said:

"Hmm, I think that I might have an idea to outsmart the giants." He looked seriously at the others. Everybody looked at Brave Hunter with expressions of expectation.

"You see", he continued, "we have to break down the dam!" He grinned when he saw the surprised faces in front of him.

"I can see you thinking; we will get an army of angry giants after us!" Brave Hunter pulled a more serious face, nodded to the king and continued:

"If we exchanged the water in the basin into Bubbly Azules Shake." The others looked at him puzzled, not quite understanding what he meant, but Brave Hunter continued quietly:

"The cocktail will make the giants happy and merry and they won't be alert anymore."

He paused for a little while to see the reaction of the others. Then he nodded to Pim and the owl:

"And then you can, together with all the animals in the forest, break down the dam. The owl thought for a while and then nodded seriously:

"If all the animals will help out, we should be able to do it."

He gave a sideways glance at the elf and asked:

"Do you have nets for us? We need nets to drag the material out of the water." The elf, who was just finishing a nut, licked his fingers and nodded fiercely. The red bob on his cap bounced back and forward.

"Yes, yes, we do have some nets in stock", he said hastily. He put his forefinger into the air and exclaimed enthusiastically:

"Tonight, I will put all the elves on the loom, so tomorrow we will have more ready." The owl nodded pleased:

"Ok, that's wonderful", and then looked at Brave Hunter with a puzzled face.

"But how do we get the Bubbly Azules Shake into the dam?" Pim nodded strongly while waving his tail back and forward.

"Yes, how are we going to get the cocktail in the basin and the water out of the basin?"

Brave Hunter looked at Norma and asked her:

"Can you change the water in the basin in

Bubbly Azules Shake?" Norma looked doubtful but then answered hesitatingly:

"Yes, basically I should be able to do that." The others were completely puzzled not understanding what they were talking about. Brave Hunter cleared his throat and explained:

"Norma is the daughter of the Mighty Sorcerer of the High Mountain and the good witch Desirée. She has inherited magical powers from her parents."

"Oh, right!", they all said in unison, while they looked at Norma in admiration.

"I had already understood that", the owl sneered in a high pitched tone.

The kobold king clapped his hands in joy and called out:

"A very good idea indeed, it is definitely worth a try." Norma threw a glance at the king and said softly:

"I can not make the water into Bubbly Azules Shake, I can only replace it."

"Oh, but that is not a problem", the king responded helpfully. He jumped out of his armchair and said to the footman:

"Drum up all the kobolds and put them to work making Bubbly Azules Shake, right away!" The footman bowed and left the hall.

Smiling the king turned to Norma while rubbing his hands.

"So, that is set Norma! Tomorrow morning

we will have plenty of Bubbly Azules Shake."
Norma smiled back.

"That is really great your majesty, but there is also something else", she said hesitantly. "In order to replace the water into Bubbly Azules Shake I have to be at the basin myself. I can not do it from this chair." Brave Hunter frowned.

"Is that really necessary? I find that a bit too dangerous." Norma nodded:

"There is no other way."

"Then I will come with you, off course!", said Brave Hunter resolutely.

Filled with excitement Neston jumped up from his chair and shouted spontaneously:

"I'll come along too, I sure would like to see the land of the giants!" But Brave Hunter shook his head.

"That is out of the question, you stay here, safe with the kobolds." But Neston was not to be put off that easily, he put his hands on his hips, tilted his head to the left and said with great determination in his voice:

"But I can be of a great help to you. I'll stand look out with my flying stick while Norma is working her magic. You see, it is not dangerous at all for me, I can always fly high up in the sky." Neston grinned: "And after all you are there to protect me, right?" Then he gestured dramatically with his hands:

"And who knows what silly things I might do when you are not around!" Brave Hunter shook his head and looked at Neston laughing.

"Ok, you have convinced me, you can come along to be our lookout."

LAUREN IS DISCOVERED

The owl jumped up from his chair.

"I think it might be wise that someone goes along with them, someone who knows the area really well." The king frowned and sat deep in thought. In the meantime Pim had been looking wide eyed at Brave Hunters rucksack, which was lying near Brave Hunter's feet.

"What on earth is going on with your rucksack? It is jumping in every direction!", he said startled.

Brave Hunter glanced down and saw that indeed his rucksack was shuffling back and forward. There was some squeaking coming out of the pack.

"Oh goodness me! We have forgotten all about Lauren!", yelled Neston.

"Lauren?", roared the king. "Lauren the kobold who is always wondering off above the earth?" Startled Alice flew to the rucksack and asked in disbelief:

"How can Lauren fit in there?" She looked at Norma and pointed. "Did you make him smaller?" Norma chuckled back at her:

"Good guess, Alice. He wanted to free us from the prison but then the bodyguard came and we had to hide him. That is why I turned him into a mouse so he could fit into Brave

Hunter's rucksack." Brave Hunter untied the rucksack and a little mouse hopped out.

"Peep, peep", it sounded through the hall. The mouse stood on his hind legs and looked at Norma with his big brown eyes.

"I think he wants to be turned back into a kobold", Pim remarked. Norma nodded and said:

"Yes, I will wiz him back straight away." She raided her hand and murmured a spell. A cloud appeared and when that had cleared Lauren stood there grinning.

The king got up from his chair.

"You have a lot to explain, young man", he said sternly, while pointing at him with his forefinger. Lauren hung his head down and mumbled softly:

"I am very sorry that I took Alice with me." He rubbed his nose and then looked straight at the king. His voice trembled:

"It would be my pleasure to show Brave Hunter the way to the basin. Nobody else knows the country above the ground as well as I do." The king rubbed his chin and said:

"Indeed, nobody gives us as much trouble as you do. Always running around above the earth doing who knows what." He squeezed his eyes together and said then decisively:

"Fine, you can be their guide." The king turned to the elf, the owl and the squirrel.

"I suggest that you go back directly to your county and get everybody together and", he gave the elf a little nod, "put them to work."

For a moment there was a silence, Brave Hunter stepped forward and announced:

"Very early in the morning, before daylight, we will substitute the water into Bubbly Azules Shake, this way you can start breaking down the dam early in the morning." All four nodded enthusiastically. The elf reacted:

"We will gather everybody at the dam at daylight." The king gestured to a footman who came straight over.

"Would you be so kind as to accompany our guests to the world above us?" The king shook the hand of the elf and the wing and paw of the owl and Pim respectively.

When they had left Brave Hunter said to the king:

"Our horses are still above the ground at the lake, we left them there in our hurry to find Alice." The king looked serious and nodded:

"I understand. Above the ground we have meadows with juicy grass and warm stables with hay and oats." He nodded resolutely.

"I will send the stable kobold to take the horses there." He just wanted to gesture to a footman to fetch the stable kobold when Brave Hunter raised his hand. He cleared his throat and said hesitantly:

"That is very kind of you king, but...", he threw a glance at Norma, "one of the horses has been turned into a dog." The king looked a little puzzled at Brave Hunter. But Brave Hunter pointed with a meaningful smile at Norma.

"This lady has turned one of the horses into a dog to search for Alice." The king nodded understanding and threw a laughing glance at Norma.

"Our luggage is at the lake", Neston said, "that has to be collected too." Brave Hunter pointed at Norma and Neston and suggested:

"If you both go with the kobold to the horses, then Norma can turn the dog back into a horse and Neston can pick up the luggage." Neston raised his eyebrows and said with an aggrieved voice:

"I can not carry that all by myself!"

"You don't have to do that", said the king quickly. "I will send two more kobolds to help you carry your luggage."

The king looked around in contentment.

"So, that is all set then. A footman will show you to the guest quarters." He clacked his tongue and turned to Brave Hunter:

"I also would like to invite you to join me for dinner tonight." Brave Hunter grinned back:

"We would be delighted of course!."

BRAM, THE GIANT CHILD, DROPS UNCONCIOUS.

Bram sat at the kitchen table. The late afternoon sun was shining through the windows. His mother stood at the kitchen sink stirring in a pan. She wore a red apron that covered a yellow dress. It smelled delicious in the kitchen.

"What time do we eat, mum?", he asked curiously. His mother turned around and waved her wooden spoon in the air.

"Around seven o'clock, your father will be home a little later today." Bram stood up.

"Then I will go to the Rock Valley for a little while to look for round stones." His mother nodded.

"That's fine, but make sure that you are home before supper." Bram grimaced:

"Don't you worry about that, mother!" His mother smiled and reacted cheerfully:

"Yes, that is true, when it comes to eating I don't have to ask twice."

She took Bram's rucksack and handed it over.

"I hope you will find some nice round stones for your collection. Please watch out for the caverns!" Bram nodded impatiently and reacted grumpily:

"I know the area like the back of my hand, mother!" His mother pulled a worried face.

"I still think that you have to be cautious, it is and always will be a dangerous area." Bram bit his under lip:

"I promise to be careful!" He put his rucksack on and went outside. The Rock Valley was just outside the Giant's village, about a half hour walking (*for a giant anyway*). Bram took large steps. He was a cheerful giant child of fourteen years and about two and a half times bigger than a human. Adult giants can grow three and a half times bigger than a human.

Bram was very fashion conscious, like all giant boys his age. He wore leather knee breeches with shining buttons on the side and a brown woollen sweater with a small zipper in it. He walked on two wooden clogs with brown cotton knee socks. He had lots of gel in his hair. Bram could spend hours in front of a mirror to style his hair. His little sister didn't understand that at all.

"I don't see any difference from when you went in", she crowed when Bram got out of the bathroom after an hour.

"Little girls don't have an eye for it", was all he said. Bram walked with big steps and pondered:

"I hope I will find a couple of rare round rocks."

In Giant's village it was a craze among the kids to play cobbles. The cobbles were kept in specially made see-through hoses, which could be bent in all kinds of directions. The more cobbles you had the longer your hose had to be, which meant that you could make nicer figures. Almost every giant boy or girl had a hose with cobbles. The game with the cobbles was actually quite easy. You took a cobble from your hose and called out loud:

"Who will make an offer for my cobble?" The person who wanted your cobble would call out:

"Take the challenge!" And you answered with:

"Show me what you've got!" The giant who had challenged you would take a cobble out of his hose. If the cobble was not to your liking you said:

"That is not a smooth rock, it looks like a smelly sock."

Then the other could do three things; take out another cobble, offer more cobbles, or leave it. When the other made a satisfying offer, you said:

"Ok, we can play." Then the real game started. A stick was stuck in the ground and from that point you took ten steps. You were the first one to throw the cobble towards the stick. Then the other one could throw his or her cobble or cobbles towards the stick. He or she could also try to nock away your cobble with his or her's. The person, whose cobble was closest to the stick, won. The winner got all the cobbles in the game. The rounder your cobble the better you could roll it and be able to aim more carefully. It would give you an advantage and thus a better chance of winning.

Bram hummed softly. He stood on the top of the mountain that bordered Giant village. The mountain pass led to a deep and steep gorge. Skilfully Bram jumped over the gorge and followed the steep path down. The path made many dizzy bends, which lead eventually into the Rock Valley. In the winter the Rock Valley and the gorge would fill up with water. Heaps of rocks and cobbles were swept from the mountains with the swirling water. That is why the valley was called 'Rock Valley'.

Bram looked around carefully. Against the mountainside was a small stack of white rocks.

"Let's have a look at that", he mumbled. He squatted down and fished a couple of cobbles from the stack and put them in his rucksack. Bram looked up towards the gorge.

"Hmm, I'm sure that there must be a pile of beautiful rocks, lying around up there", he pondered. His parents had always forbidden him from going into the gorge.

"Way too many dangerous cracks and loose

lying rock blocks!", his father always said severely. Bram whistled through his lips and thought:

"Oh, it won't hurt if I just walk in for a short distance."

Fearlessly he walked into the gorge, scrambling over a couple of rock blocks. After a short distance he saw in a dry creek bed a big beautiful smooth round cobble. He jumped down the big boulder and picked it up with both hands. He kissed the rock and yelled out joyfully:

"You are a jewel!" His new acquisition was put into the rucksack together with the other rocks. There were more beautiful examples scattered and quickly Bram filled up his rucksack. The pack had become so heavy that he had to hold it with both hands.

"Time to go home", he said softly to himself.

He had to get back on top of the rock block he had jumped off, to get back. But because of the heavy rucksack he couldn't scramble over so easily. He stepped on some smaller stones and wanted to put the rucksack on the large rock. He stood on the top of his wooden shoes and hung forward a little. But the small stones under him started to roll and Bram lost his balance. With the heavy bag in his right-hand, Bram fell backwards. His head hit a rock and

he fell to the ground unconscious.

"Why isn't Bram home yet?", his mother wondered worried. His father had been home for a while. Everyone was sitting at the dinner table. His sister Lisa and his brother Yuri were getting impatient.

"Can't we start eating, mum?", Yuri asked impatiently. "I am starving!"

"Yes, go ahead", his father answered. "Bram will be home any moment." Mother looked doubtful.

"It is not like Bram to be so late." She put the dishes on the table, sat down and started to serve.

"I hope nothing terrible happened", she sighed. Father took a big bite and shook his head.

"Don't be so gloomy. He will stick his head around the corner any moment now."

But when everybody had finished eating and mother had cleared the table, Bram still hadn't showed up. Father stood up and threw a meaningful glance at his wife.

"I am going out to find him." Mother nodded and frowned.

"Good idea, I am really getting worried." Father took his coat and a lantern and walked outside.

It was dead quite in the street. All the giants were at home eating or playing board games. Soft light was shining behind the windows. Father pulled the collar of his coat a little higher. He lit the lantern and walked into the direction of the Rock valley. When he finally reached the mountain pass he still hadn't come across Bram. Now he really started to worry.

"I hope he didn't go to the gorge and fall down a crack", he thought in fright. It was now too dark to jump the pass by himself, so he walked quickly back to the village to get some help.

He pounded his big fist on his neighbour's front door.

"Open up, hurry!", he roared. The neighbour shuffled to the door, opened it and asked in surprise:

"What's going on?" Bram's father gestured impatiently:

"Hurry up, we have to look for Bram; he is missing." The neighbour quickly grabbed his coat and a lantern and walked outside. They stopped at some more houses. And so a party of giants carrying lanterns; went to the Rock Valley.

"Bram, Bram where are you?", they called out. The giants were criss-crossing through the valley. But there was not a single sign of Bram.

"Could he have walked into the gorge?",
suggested one of the giants. The father of Bram
shook his head.

"I have warned him over and over again not
to go in there." The neighbour walked over and
said calmly:

"It might be possible that he has gone in
there, anyway." Another giant reacted grinding
on his teeth:

"That would be really stupid." The neighbour
made a sidelong glance at Bram's father.

"It is too dark to go in now. We will come
back tomorrow at the crack of dawn." The other
giants nodded in agreement.

"That is a good idea", one said.

"Yes it is now way too dark to go in", said
another. Bram's father put on a sullen face and
muttered:

"Apparently there is no other solution." His
neighbour threw his arm around him and said
encouraging:

"Don't you worry, we will find him tomorrow
for sure."

THE NIGHT ADVENTURE

"That was a delicious meal, king", sighted Brave Hunter contently while stretching his arms in the air.

"Hmm, indeed, those chocolate truffles are especially yummy!", Neston said cheerfully, while licking his lips. Alice gave him a tap on his fingers.

"That is very rude you know, licking your fingers!" She looked apologetically at the king. The king laughed:

"I am glad that you like it so much." Brave Hunter shuffled his chair back and got up.

"It is long past bedtime." The king clacked his tongue startled:

"Rubies in a pile, it's already ten o' clock! At what time do you need the Bubbly Azules Shake?" Brave hunter scratched himself behind the ear thought deeply and answered:

"Hmm, let's see, I want to give you as much time as possible."

After a couple of minutes he looked at the king and proposed:

"We will substitute the water with the Bubbly Azules Shake very early in the morning. This will give us enough time to get away before the giants wake up." The king nodded in agreement. Brave Hunter rubbed his hands and yawned:

"Fine, we will leave here just after midnight."
The king sighed deeply and got up:

"I will check on the kobolds, to see how far
they are along with the preparation of the
cocktails." He said seriously, while shaking
Brave Hunter's hand:

"I wish you luck and be careful!" Then he
turned to Norma.

"And to this little witch, I wish you all the
magic in the world." Then he turned to Lauren
and said in a friendly but worried tone:

"Make sure that they don't get lost, Lauren!"
Lauren swallowed and stuttered shyly.

"I will do my best, king." Then he gave
Neston a pat on the shoulder and gave him a
wink with his left eye:

"Take good care of those three." Neston
blushed and stammered:

"Yes your majesty."

When the king had left, Brave Hunter looked
at the others and proposed:

"I suggest that we all get some sleep now, I
will wake you up around midnight." He made a
grimace at Alice. "Don't you worry, I won't wake
you up little princes." Alice stretched her arms
in the air and yawned:

"I have to confess that I am very, very tired.
So much has happened today!"

Just after midnight the group was standing at the underground lake.

"So, this is where they gather the water?", asked Neston while he looked with big eyes at the waterwheel with the jars. Lauren nodded and walked down the stairs to the landing.

"Yes, and behind the landing lays our rowing boat." Lauren bent over and pulled the cords to which the boat was tied. He gestured with his hand.

"Please, get on board." Norma stepped in first and sat in the front of the boat. Brave Hunter took his place in the back. Lauren and Neston both sat in the middle and each took an oar. Neston pushed the boat from the landing and put his oar in the water.

The splash of their oars sounded over the water. They only had to stroke for a few minutes to cross the lake and then sailed along the underground river.

Because there were not many glow-worms, it was pretty dark.

"Norma, please can you wiz us up some lanterns", Brave Hunter called out to her. Within a wink Brave Hunter and Norma had a lantern in their hands. Norma's was shining on the wall. They were full of moss and dark crevices. She felt a shiver running down her spine. It was quite damp and cold. The boat was gliding quickly through the water. Lauren

and Neston were really pulling on the oars. After a while Norma saw a fork in the distance. She held the lantern above her head and squinted into the dark.

"The river is dividing here!", she said in surprise to the others.

"That is correct", said Lauren. "To the right, the river is going to the giant's dam and to the left the river is going to our diamond mines." He turned his head backwards and threw a glance at Norma.

"And we are going to the left." Neston glanced sideways at Lauren and asked wondering:

"Why are we going to the mines? I thought we had to go as quickly as possible to the dam?"

Lauren threw an impatient glance at Neston and said:

"Of course we are going there, what do you think!" Neston shrugged his shoulders.

"I just don't get it. It seemed more logical to me if we get as close as to the dam as possible. And that would be to the right and now we are sailing towards the mines." He pushed his oars a little deeper in the water.

"No doubt the mines lie under the Giant village", suggested Brave Hunter, while he looked at Lauren inquisitively. Lauren smiled, nodded and responded:

"That is right, this way we can approach the dam more easily."

When they had rowed for a half hour or more they arrived at a little dock. Brave Hunter tied the boat to the dock, while the others were getting out. At the end of the dock was a gate. Lauren opened it and was followed by Neston, Norma and Brave Hunter.

They arrived in some sort of hallway. There were tables and chairs and a corner that looked like a little kitchen.

"This is where the mineworkers have lunch at midday", explained Lauren, while he continued walking. The others still followed him. They walked into some sort of station, where there were a dozen, two-person pedal trains, standing on a rail. Lauren pointed at the pedal trains.

"These trains will bring us to the heart of the mines and near the Giant village." He stepped into a wagon and gestured at Neston to sit beside him. Brave Hunter and Norma stepped into the wagon behind them.

The minute they were out of the hallway they found themselves in a dark tunnel. The light of the lanterns, which Norma and Neston were holding, reflected against the rock side. Their shadows danced on the wall.

"What is that over there?", asked Neston in

surprise, while he pointed at a spot of light in the distance.

"That is the emerald mine", responded Lauren cheerfully. "We have four sorts of mines: the emerald mine, the diamond mine, the ruby mine and the sapphire mine." They rode into the emerald mine. It was a large space with several wooden bins. A couple of alleys lead to the room. In the centre of the room were several water tanks. All kinds of working tools hung on the wall. They quickly rode through it and continued into another dark tunnel. The next mine was a ruby mine with three corridors leading to it. They took the corridor on the right. And again they were peddling in a dark tunnel. The tunnel had all kinds of crooked bends. Eventually they came to a small round room.

Lauren stopped the wagon.

"From this point we have to go by foot", he said, while he got out of his carriage.

"Brr, it's a gloomy place", whispered Norma, while she trotted behind Lauren. They walked into a small niche with a door. Lauren opened the door and they saw a ladder hanging down.

"This ladder ends at the border of Giant village", said Lauren softly while he pointed upwards. Lauren put is forefinger to his lips and whispered:

"If I am not mistaken, the giants will still be

in their beds. But still we have to be as quiet as possible." Brave Hunter nodded and said in a whispered voice:

"I will go first." He took the cords of the ladder and climbed up. He could see an opening above his head. He stuck his head through it, inhaled fresh night air and sighted contently:

"Hmm, this is sure refreshing."

It was a clear night, the stars and the moon in the sky lit up the landscape. Brave Hunter looked around him. In a distance he saw the houses of the giants. Dawn was just starting to break. All of Giant village was still sound asleep.

"Hey, we also want to go up", Neston said to Brave Hunter in a soft voice.

"Yes, yes, I will climb up now", whispered Brave Hunter. He put his hands on the ground and pushed himself up.

"Hmm, even the grass seemed much larger here", Brave Hunter thought when he finally stood above the ground.

In the meantime Neston had also climbed up.

"Hmm, fresh air", he sniffed, when he put his head above the ground. In a jiffy he stood next to Brave Hunter on the grass. "I really feel very small now", said Neston excitedly, while he stared at the giant houses. Brave Hunter took off his rucksack and took out the case of mother-of-pearls. He sprinkled some magic powder on to Neston's hair and did the same with himself. In an eye-blink they were back to their old size. Neston stretched himself and yawned:

"I still feel very small, you know, the houses are so huge." Lauren who was now standing next to him, slapped him on the shoulder and said laughing:

"They are called giants for a reason." Norma, who had climbed after Lauren waved her arms, a cloud appeared. When the cloud had disappeared Norma was standing in front of them; her normal size again.

"We are now south of the village", explained Lauren. "Come on, we have to go that way to the dam", he gestured.

Quietly the group walked behind Lauren. After a quarter of an hour they arrived at a high brick wall with stairs cut into it. They climbed up the staircase, leading to a platform on top of the wall. On the platform a small stone fence surrounded the dam. This fence separated them from the water. Norma looked at the basin with large eyes .

"What a large dam and what a huge pool of water", she said with a high pitched voice. "I sure hope that the kobolds have made enough Bubbly Azules Shake." Brave Hunter untied

his rucksack and took out a bottle and gave that to Norma.

"Here you go Norma, the bottle with the Bubbly Azules Shake." Norma took the bottle and unscrewed it. She let a drop fall on her finger, licked it and nodded approvingly. She turned the bottle over and let the cocktail pour into the water while she murmured.

"Basin fill up right now,
from this bottle some how.
Water so clear,
be gone – disappear!"

For a couple of minutes the dam was covered in a foggy mist. But when the fog had cleared, they could see that the water in the dam was gone and a big black cloud hung above it.

Then it started to blow very, very strongly, as if a storm was announcing itself. The wind was blowing around their ears and Norma's hair was fluttering straight backwards in the wind. The group had to hold on tight to the stony fence that ran around the dam. The cloud drifted towards Kobold land and from the opposite direction another cloud appeared, driving towards them. When that cloud was hanging above the basin the wind stopped as suddenly as it had started.

"I almost blew away", shouted Neston in a fright to the others when the wind had calmed down. "It seemed like a local hurricane!" But Norma kept her eyes focused on the cloud that was hanging above the basin. She put both her hands forward and with closed eyes she started to mumble. Suddenly the cloud started pouring cats and dogs and in a couple of seconds the basin was filled with the Bubbly Azules Shake. The blue drink bubbled swirling in the basin and the scent of carrot-extract filled the air.

"It worked!", exclaimed Norma relieved and she looked beaming at the others.

"Indeed, well done Norma", complemented Lauren. But suddenly Neston said startled:

"I see giants in a distance walking towards us!" The others turned their heads around and saw that indeed a group of giants were walking their way.

"Quickly back to the mines", Lauren said flustered, while waving heatedly with his arms. But it was too late, because the giants took large steps and were coming closer and closer. Tensely Brave Hunter looked around him, then gestured to a bunch of bushes and yelled:

"Quick, let's go there in the bushes!" In a flash the group ran down the stairs and hid in the bushes. They were just good and well hidden when they heard the deep voices of the giants.

"Boy, they are really big!", Neston thought in amazement. He pinched his arm. "No, I am not dreaming"

"Don't worry, we will find Bram", they heard one of the giants say to the others.

"He can't have disappeared from the earth", another giant grumbled. The giants passed the bush. A giant child ran in front of the others.

"Be careful Yuri!", roared a big giant to the giant child.

"I will go ahead to fill our water bags", Yuri yelled back at them. After a couple of seconds they heard Yuri scream:

"What happened to the water?" In a jiffy the other giants got to the dam. One giant kneeled down and scooped some cocktail into his hand and gulped it down.

"Sure tastes good", he said surprised to the others. Now the other giants kneeled down to taste the Shake.

One big giant frowned and look worried.

"There are sure strange things happening. First Bram disappears and now this. What is going on?"

ALICE MEETS BRAM

Dawn was just breaking when Alice woke up. She looked at the empty bed across the room.

"Norma has not come back yet", she thought. She got out of bed and walked to the bathroom. "A good bath does miracles for a fairy", she whistled gaily, while filling up the bath. When she had washed and dressed herself, she walked to the dining room where they had eaten yesterday.

It was really dead quiet in the palace, nobody to be seen or heard. Alice walked into the room and whispered softly to herself:

"Hmm, of course the king must still be sleeping. No doubt you get very tired after a long night of making drinks."

"That is correct", said a voice behind her. It was the same footman who had served them yesterday. He stood in the doorway and continued:

"The last drop of Bubbly Azules Shake was made a couple of hours ago. Then everyone went straight to their beds."

The footman walked a little further into the room and then asked:

"What may I bring you for breakfast?" With

his left-hand he counted off the fingers of his right and said:

"Orange juice, milk, tea, bread, fruit." Alice wet her lips and said enthusiastically:

"That sounds delicious, thank you." She walked to the table and sat down. For a little moment the footman hesitated.

"Does she wants to have it all?", he thought both in shock and surprise. But because Alice didn't react, he walked back to the kitchen, shaking his head.

"Are the others back already?", asked the cook bewildered when the footman listed the breakfast. He shrugged his shoulders and shook his head:

"No, it is all for the little fairy." The cook raised his head and pulled a comical face. Ten minutes later the footman was back in the dining room with a tray.

"Is Brave Hunter back already?", asked Alice, when the footman put the can with orange juice on the table.

"No, nobody has come back yet." Alice pulled a face and asked in concern:

"They should have been back already, right?" She looked at him inquisitively while he was putting the buns of bread on the table. He nodded and answered:

"Yes, I would have expected them to be back long ago."

"Maybe they are helping the animals to break down the dam", pondered Alice. Then she said suddenly:

"I think, I will fly and find them after breakfast. Do you have a map of the area?", she asked, while grabbing a bun from the basket.

"Off course, I will get one right away", he answered with a smile.

By the time he came back with the map, Alice had feasted on the delicious breakfast. The jar with orange juice was half empty and most of the buns had been consumed. He spread the map over the table. He pointed to a green spot and said:

"Look, this is the exit, I will take you there." Alice looked up and smiled at him.

"That is very kind of you." The footman blushed a little, while smiling back at her, but then continued his story, while still pointing at the map.

"From this spot it is easiest to follow the gorge. And since you can fly, the obstacles, such as the cracks in the ground and the big rock blocks, won't bother you. Just at the end of the gorge you must turn to the right. If I am not mistaken, you will see a river. Follow the river downstream and you are bound to run into the bottom of the dam." He folded up the map and gave it to Alice.

"Let me know when you want to leave." Alice

jumped up enthusiastically from her chair and said:

"Shall we leave now?"

They had been walking quite a while. The footman had shepherded Alice criss cross through the underground corridors. Alice didn't have a clue where they were. They were now standing next to a staircase.

"I am very sorry but I have to return to the palace", he said with a little regret in his voice. Alice nodded timidly.

"It is a pity, it would have been great if you would have come along, but I do understand. Thank you so much for bringing me all the way to the exit. I would have walked in circles otherwise. All those corridors seem the same." Then she flew up, waved her hand and said warmly:

"See you tonight!" The footman smiled, waved back and turned around.

When Alice reached the surface, the sun had just started to climb higher and higher. She squinted in the intense light.

"My, the sun seems bright, after being under ground so long", she thought. She put her hand above her eyes and gazed into the distance. "The gorge must be over there", she said softly to herself, while she flew in that direction.

And indeed, after a little while she reached a valley. The whole valley was covered with all sorts of rocks. Alice looked around with interest and mumbled:

"It is quite barren here." She flew across the valley and passed the big rock that was blocking the gorge.

"I hope that Brave Hunter, Norma and Neston are not too far away", she thought hopefully. Suddenly she heard somebody groaning in pain. She put her ear to the ground and started to fly more slowly.

When she flew over a very large stone she saw Bram lying on the ground, leaning against a rock. In fright she hid behind the stone. Her heart was pounding in her throat.

"Help, a giant!", Alice whispered shocked. Bram's groaning was getting louder and louder.

"Ouch, ouch, I am in such pain", he moaned. Alice peeked around the stone and saw Bram pulling a painful face. She thought feverishly.

"It looks as if the giant is in a lot of pain and there is nobody around to help him." Alice rubbed her chin.

"You can't leave him lying there, Alice!", a small voice within her said sternly.

"Oh yes you can, it's a trick", said another internal voice.

Alice shook her head firmly and fluttered her

wings, which set off the little bells and then flew resolutely to Bram. He looked in surprise at the little creature that was flying above him.

"Hi, I am Alice", she said to the startled giant. Bram stammered back:

"And I I I, I aaaaam Bram."

"Have you hurt yourself?", asked Alice concerned. Bram bit on his bottom lip and nodded.

"Indeed, I fell yesterday and I think I have sprained my ankle." His right-hand was supporting his left ankle.

"I can't stand up on it." He looked at Alice with a pained face.

"I had thought that my parents would have found me by now." He shrugged his shoulders, "but until now I have not seen a soul." Then his face cleared up and he asked curiously: "You are a fairy, aren't you? I have never seen a fairy before." Alice nodded smiling and then asked seriously:

"You have been lying here since last night? That is quite long."

Alice thought for a moment and said:

"I can't leave you here of course but how do I get you out of the gorge?" Alice looked worried but Bram gestured with his hands:

"If you roll those two tree trunks over here I can use them as crutches." He made a grimace. "And then I can hop out of the gorge."

Alice lifted her arm, flexed her biceps and said chuckling:

"Yes, I'll just lift it up in a snap, no problem!" Bram laughed and replied:

"Yes, you are right, it is not that easy." He looked a little more serious and asked: "Could you warn my parents that I am lying here?" Alice brought her finger to her mouth but then shook her little head.

"No, I can't do that for you, but I can get help." Alice fluttered her wings. "I promise I will be back in a flash with help." She waved cheerfully to Bram and swiftly flew away.

It was about a half hour flying to the end of the gorge. She turned to the right and soon she heard a hum of voices in the distance. The voices came from elves, dragging nets behind them. A little further down she saw rabbits, hares and other animals walking with all kinds of sticks, branches and wood. Then she saw Pim running past the rabbits with a bag of sand. She waved joyfully to Pim.

"Well, good morning Alice," said Pim in surprise and asked:

"Are you going to help us to break up the dam?" Alice made a little jump in the air and laughed:

"I was too curious to stay in the palace." She looked inquisitively at Pim.

"Are Brave Hunter, Norma, Lauren and

Neston here?" Pim shook his head and answered:

"No, I have not seen them here. But we do know that Norma managed to replace the water with the Bubbly Azules Shake. I had sent a couple of kobolds over there to investigate and they had seen that the giants were very cheerful." He grimaced at Alice. "They are so busy celebrating, that we can break up the dam, down here, undisturbed." Alice gave a sigh of relief.

"I am glad that it has worked."

Then she looked more seriously at Pim and said nervously.

"I need help Pim." Pim looked questioningly at Alice. "Well, you see", Alice started, "on my way here, I flew into a giant who has sprained his ankle. I was wondering if you could spare some elves to roll a couple of tree trunks to him, so he can hop out of the gorge. I feel so sorry for him. He has been there since last night!" Alice looked tensely at Pim. He looked doubtful and frowned.

"Hmm, I don't fancy that at all. But I suppose I can't leave the giant lying there." He waved to an elf to come over. "Where is your doctor?", he asked the elf.

"With the diggers", was the answer.

"Could you fetch him together with nine strong elves?" The elf snapped his fingers.

"I will go straight away!"

Within thirty minutes ten elves were standing around Bram.

"Please let me pass", said the doctor impatiently. He was carrying a big black bag. "We will first take your shoe off." He tried to pull a lace, but there was no movement at all.

"Those laces seem like thick cables", sighed the doctor while he hung on to the lace.

"Wait, I will take it off myself", Bram said quickly. Frightened, the doctor stuffed his fingers in his ears.

"Can't you talk a little bit more quietly, we are not deaf you know!" He looked sternly at Bram and roared on: "Because otherwise we will become deaf!" Bram whispered quickly:

"Sorry", and took off his sock. The doctor looked with a worried face and growled:

"Hmm, that doesn't look too good." He opened up the bag and took out a roll of greased cotton wool and some bandages. "I will bandage your ankle - it will reduce the swelling and the pain", he yelled to the giant.

While the doctor was putting the cotton on the ankle, Alice gave Bram something to eat and to drink.

"Hmm, Hmm", mumbled Bram contently. "I didn't realise how hungry I was!"

When Bram's ankle had been bandaged, the elves rolled the tree trunks to him. Carefully Bram tried to get up. Because of the compressive bandage the pain was much less. After a couple of attempts he stood on one leg, with the two trunks under his arm. He looked cheerfully around him and said shyly:

"Thank you very, very much, without your help I still would be lying here." Then he bent forward to Alice and said softly:

"And I am most grateful to this little fairy." Alice laughed shyly. Bram leaned on the right trunk and swung his left leg back and forward.

"I must quickly go back to my mother and father, they must be worried sick." Bram looked at the others: "And if ever I can do anything in return?"

Alice frowned a little and flew to the doctor. She whispered something in his ear. He mumbled:

"Yes, yes, you are right, that is a good idea." The doctor looked up at the giant and called out to him:

"There is a way you can help us. Could you please come along with us now?" Bram looked surprised and asked bewildered:

"Right now?" The doctor nodded and said decisively:

"Yes, right now." Bram looked around in confusion and stuttered:

"But, but, I have to go first to my parents, because they don't have a clue where I am." The doctor shook his head.

"I will send somebody to you parents with a message." He waved impatiently to the giant. Bram didn't know what to do. Follow the doctor or go back home? After some hesitation he decided to follow the doctor. After all they had helped him splendidly. The doctor nodded satisfied.

He didn't want Bram to go back to Giant village, because then their plan to break up the dam would be endangered. That was why Alice had flown to the doctor with the idea to take Bram with them. And so the group of elves, giant and fairy walked on.

PANIC IN GIANT VILLAGE

In the meantime, Brave Hunter, Neston, Norma and Lauren were still in Giant village. Soon after the giants had discovered that the basin was filled with Bubbly Azules Shake, giants came running from every corner. There was a very busy, lively cheerful hive of activity. Every giant wanted to taste the cocktail. A couple of giants were singing, while one giant played his flute. Here and there, some giants were dancing.

Near the bushes where our friends hid, were a group of female giants.

"What has happened?", they heard one woman ask startled. Another woman giant answered:

"It seems that the water in the dam has changed into some delicious blue shake." The woman slipped her hand in front of her mouth and asked in surprise:

"How can that have happened?" The other giant shrugged her shoulders and answered:

"I have no idea."

"Has the king been warned?", someone asked.

"Yes, he has a meeting this morning with his ministers and some scholars", was the answer.

At that very same moment the king was sitting in the meeting-room of his palace together with his five ministers and three scholars.

"It is a clear case of acute aqua humoritus", noted a scholar giant with round glasses on his nose. The other scholars nodded fiercely.

"There is no doubt about it", agreed another scholar.

"Yes, a case of acute aqua humoritus", said the third scholar with a deep voice. The king looked at them frowning.

"Acute aqua humoritus? What do I have to picture then?" The scholar with the round glasses took of his glasses. He rubbed his eye with his left hand and said weightily:

"When a cold water current mixes with a warm water current, you get a chemical reaction." The other two scholars nodded strongly.

"That's right", they said affirmatively.

"So tonight a cold water current from the mountain, has blended in with the warm current from our village", continued the scholar.

For a little while it was quiet in the room.

"And what can we do about it?", the king finally asked.

"We have to consult about that", the scholars said almost in unison. Then one minister stood up in anger.

"What nonsense: warm water current, cold water current", he raved to the scholars, while he stormed up and down the room. "Really, that is sheer nonsense." He looked with anger at the scholar with the round   glasses. The scholar turned a deep shade of red and stuttered:

"This, this.......is scientifically explained." The minister looked straight at him and replied:

"How strange, I have never heard of it before. It is very coincidental that a warm water stream is running so smoothly to our village! Where would that have been coming from?" He hit the table with his fist. The scholars gathered their papers nervously and got up.

"We are going to consult now, your majesty, about solving this urgent problem", stuttered the scholar with the glasses to the king. They made a little bow and quickly walked out of the room.

The king leaned back in his chair and said with an authoritative voice:

"Jan, please sit down." Jan shuffled his chair backwards and took his place at the table. He looked around and asked the others:

"You surely don't believe this story of a warm current and cold current, do you?" A minister with a pointy beard raised his forefinger.

"Ah, hum, I do think that it could be possible if you look at all aspects of the situation while taking into account the available facts."

Jan looked bewildered at the minister and raged:

"What are you spluttering about?" He then turned to the king and said sharply:

"It is of course the revenge of the kobolds, the elves and the animals of the forest." The king looked at him with large eyes. Jan leaned forward over the table.

"I have been telling you for months that we are too greedy", he said fiercely. "But nobody wanted to listen to me."

"After all, the water is ours", said a fat minister in loud voice. Jan started to turn red in anger and strongly shook his head.

"Of course not, the water is for everybody!"

The king smacked his lips and remarked:

"Because of the dam we have water, all year round."

"Precisely", squeaked a minister with a high collar, exuberantly. "In the old days we had periods in the summer when it didn't rain much and there would be hardly any water. Because of the basin we now have water all year round."

"That is correct, but the price we ask for it is

way too high." He looked straight at the king. "I suggest that we have a meeting with the F.J.E Council." The king reflected in a clear voice:

"Hmm, do you realise what that would mean?" He looked penetratingly at Jan who nodded and answered cynically:

"Yes, it would mean that we have to do some things ourselves again." The fat minister banged his fist on the table and raged:

"The construction of the dam has cost a lot of time and effort." The minister with the pointy beard nodded and stuttered:

"Yes correct, a lot of effort."

Jan looked at the fat minister and roared back:

"Asking a small price is not the issue, but the large contribution we demand is way out of line." He put his hands to his face in despair and said:

"Don't you get it?" The fat minister put his hand on his belly and said in a smooth voice:

"We will see to it that they don't get any water at all." He laughed meanly and chuckled:

"That will make them come to their senses in no time!" The king nodded approving:

"Yes, let us start with that." Jan looked at the king in astonishment and asked baffled:

"Are you not going to change anything at all?" The king sighed heavily.

"It is not all that easy." He looked intensely

at Jan and said with a low voice:

"And in any case we can never ever let ourselves be blackmailed by anyone." Jan took his coat and dashed furiously out of the room.

Deep in thought Jan walked through the village. He just couldn't understand why the king and the other ministers were so headstrong.

"Good morning, Uncle Jan", he heard somebody call out. It was his little nephew Yuri, who was sitting on a large rock having a picnic. Jan waved to Yuri and walked over to him.

"Good morning to you too, Yuri", he said with a smile.

"Do you want to have a sandwich?", Yuri asked his uncle.

"Hmm, you don't have to ask me twice, I feel quite hungry", answered Jan, while he sat next to Yuri on the rock.

Yuri handed him over a sandwich with cheese and a glass of milk. Jan took a gulp out of the glass.

"Hmm, really nice", he said with a sigh, while rubbing off his milk moustache with the back of his hand.

"But, why are you actually sitting here having a picnic?", he asked puzzled at Yuri. Yuri, who just had taken a big bite out of his sandwich, chewed hastily. When his mouth was almost empty he answered:

"Bram did not come home last night, Uncle Jan." Jan nodded slowly and said calmly:

"Yes, I have heard something about it." Yuri pointed at a group of giants who were singing cheerfully and said:

"The minute they stop drinking, we will go to the gorge to search for Bram. I am just waiting for them to get ready."

He threw his uncle a sidelong glance.

"Do you know who has done this, Uncle Jan?" Jan sighed, while nodding his head.

"I think it has been done by the elves, kobolds and the animals in the forest. You see, they have to do a lot of work for us." Yuri looked inquisitively at his uncle, who pointed at his clothes and explained:

"In exchange for that, they get water." Yuri frowned and asked:

"And is the king going to change that now?", Uncle Jan shook his head.

"No, the king is too head-strong." Yuri looked up at his uncle.

"But you don't approve of that hey, Uncle Jan?" Uncle Jan shook his head cautiously and answered:

"No, I don't approve at all."

"Hi. Yuri there you are!", shouted his father

to him.

"When are we going to search for Bram, dad?", asked Yuri when his father stood before him.

"I think it is going to be just you and me boy, the others are too busy celebrating", answered his father. Yuri jumped up from the rock.

"Finally", he said gladly. He turned around and asked his uncle:

"Are you coming along with us, Uncle Jan?" Jan smiled and said without hesitation:

"Off course I am going to help you search." Yuri threw a glance at his picnic basket.

"Put that behind the bushes, Yuri", his father suggested, while pointing at the bushes where Brave Hunter and the others were hiding. The group held their breath when they saw Yuri approaching. Yuri chucked the large basket under the bushes and walked back to the other giants. Fortunately, he had not noticed them.

IN SEARCH OF BRAM

The three giants had walked quite far into the gorge, but there was still no sign of Bram.

"Where can he be?", his father grumbled anxiously. "I can't imagine that he has walked this far into the gorge." Uncle Jan, half closed his eyes, gazed into the distance and proposed:

"I think we have to keep on searching a little bit further, just to make sure."

"Yes dad", Yuri said with a lot of tension in his voice, "maybe he got lost." His father looked at him and said with a clear voice:

"Off course we'll keep on searching, I was just surprised that we had not encountered Bram yet." He turned to his brother: "I had expected that he would have been at the beginning of the gorge, with a sprained ankle or something. It is such a treacherous area." Uncle Jan nodded and said hesitantly:

"It is indeed a bit peculiar", but then he continued: "Come on, we will find him for sure. Forward march, giants!" And so it was that the three giants climbed further.

Just a little bit further down the road Bram was sitting in the sun, against a rock block. The two tree trunks were lying neatly on each side of him. Alice sat on his left shoulder. Both were looking at the animals and elves, who were busy dragging sand, rock and clay. Alice just had told Bram the whole story about the fact that the animals, elves and kobolds couldn't meet the giant's demands anymore. And that, that was the reason why they had switched the water in the dam into Bubbly Azules Shake, so the giants would not notice when they were breaking down the dam.

Bram sighed deeply:

"I had no idea we made you work so hard." He tilted his head a little bit to the left so he could see Alice sitting. "I heard my uncle talking about it sometimes." He shook his head. "But I never actually gave it a thought." Sadly Bram looked at the busy animals and elves in front of them.

"The giants can fix the dam in a couple of days. I am afraid that this won't do much good." Alice flew from his shoulder and asked in panic:

"But what must we do then?" Bram didn't answer and stared in the distance.

After a little while he broke the silence.

"I will talk with my uncle about it. Maybe he can discuss it with the king and those dreadful giants who call themselves ministers." Bram raised his eyebrows and said scornfully:"But I doubt that it will make any difference."

"There are giants coming! Giants are coming this way!", a rabbit yelled out in fright, while he passed them running. The other animals and elves had also heard him yelling. In no time a large group was gathered around the rabbit, who was standing on his two hind legs, gesturing wildly.

"I was looking for a nice sweet carrot", said the rabbit. "So I walked along the river and then I heard voices. At first I thought: *Great, extra help is on the way*, but when they came closer it turned out to be three giants. And they are coming this way!" The little rabbit looked scared and whispered:

"I don't know what you guys are going to do, but I sure want to get the hell out of here!"

And poof, the little rabbit scooted away into the direction of the meadows. The little rabbit had hardly spoken his last sentence when all the other animals and elves started running for their lives, away from the dam and the river. Within a few seconds the whole area was abandoned.

Alice, who was sitting on Bram's shoulder, looked around with big wide eyes and asked:

"Where can I go?" Bram nodded and said in calm voice:

"Stay where you are, you will be safe."

Not much later they heard the voices of a couple of giants.

"Hey, that is my father's voice", said Bram pleasantly surprised. "And I also hear my brother's voice!" Bram put his hands to his mouth and yelled:

"Yo ho, yo ho, I am here!" Immediately he heard an answer.

"It is Bram!", they heard a giant say joyfully. And indeed they saw three giants approaching in the bend of the river. Bram waved enthusiastically with his arms. The three giants waved back exuberantly.

"I am so glad that we found you!", yelled Bram's father gladly.

"I have sprained my ankle!", Bram yelled back. The three giants came walking towards Bram with big steps.

"What kept you?", asked Bram when they were standing in front of him.

"It was too dark last night to enter the gorge", his father answered. Then he looked sternly at Bram.

"How often have I told you not to go in there!" Bram nodded shamefully.

"Who bandaged your ankle?", his uncle asked in surprise, while pointing at the bandages that was wrapped around Bram's ankle. Bram's face lit up.

"I ran into Alice, or I should say, Alice flew

into me." He chuckled and pointed at Alice. The three other giants followed his finger and saw Alice crouched on Bram's shoulder. Alice was clearly very impressed by the large giants. She had thought that Bram was large, but his father and uncle were much larger. Shyly she hid behind Bram's neck.

"And she bandaged your ankle?", his uncle asked hesitantly. Bram shook his head.

"No, no, Alice got help."

Yuri, who had never seen a fairy before, stared at Alice in amazement.

"Are there more fairies?", he asked impressed. Bram tilted his head back and laughed:

"No, there aren't any more fairies. Alice is from Jingleland and on her way to Wizard County." The others looked at him inquisitively.

"What is she doing here then?", Yuri wanted to know. Bram scratched his throat and gestured to the other giants to sit down.

"Brave Hunter, Alice's friend, got a letter from his uncle in Corsica", he started his story. Alice nodded fiercely, while she fluttered with her wings, you could hear the little bells tingle, and continued:

"Yes, that is right, Brave Hunter's uncle has been attacked several times by the pirates."

The giants looked intensely at Alice, who was telling all the details of the story. She told about the pirates, the mean wicked witches, who had put the fairies in little glass jars and how Brave Hunter had helped them. She told about the trip to Norma's father the Mighty Sorcerer of the High Mountain. Then she told how she was taken by the kobold, Lauren, to the county under the earth. In detail she reported about the ceremony and the gathering of the council.

Uncle Jan nodded and mumbled under his breath.

"I knew it. I knew that they were behind it." Bram looked at his uncle with fixed attention.

"I had no idea we exploited the animals, kobolds and elves to this extent. Why haven't you done anything about it, Uncle Jan?", Bram wanted to know. Uncle Jan shrugged his shoulders despondently.

"I have warned the king and the other ministers over and over again. They just would not listen." He looked at the others one by one and said resolutely:

"But now it's gone too far. They will have to listen!" It was quiet for a while.

"But", Bram's father suddenly said cheerfully, "first, we will bring this giant-lad home." Bram grabbed the two trunks as the other giants helped him to get up. Alice who was still sitting on Bram's shoulder, stammered:

"I think I will fly back now to the kobolds."

Uncle Jan looked at Alice and asked:

"Could you ask the members of the F.J.E. Council to be at the Clover bridge at seven o'clock tonight? I would like to talk to them." Alice nodded and answered:

"Yes, sure, I will ask them that." Uncle Jan rubbed his hands and said cheerfully:

"Great, then I will make sure that the king will be there too."

Bram who was leaning on the tree-trunks looked shyly at Alice.

"Again I want to thank you for helping me. I hope you stop by, before you go on your way to Wizard County." Alice waved back:

"I won't leave without saying goodbye to you!" And then she flew away.

THE GIANT'S ASSIGNMENT.

It was all hustle and bustle in Kobold County. Kobolds were talking loudly in the square about the dam and the giants. In the palace the members of the F.J.E Council were gathered toge-ther. It was dead quiet, nobody said a word. Everyone was busy with their own thoughts. The elf who sat sprawled in an arm-chair, suddenly bounced up.

"Is Brave Hunter back all ready?" The king shook his head.

"I don't think so." He gestured to the footman at the door, who walked immediately towards the king.

"Is Brave Hunter already back from Giant County?", he asked. The footman nodded and answered:

"Yes, I think so, your majesty, I think he has just returned." The king looked wide-eyed and said impatiently:

"Bring him in immediately!"

In a hurry the footman left the room to fetch Brave Hunter. He returned with Brave Hunter within a couple of minutes. .

"Good day, your Royal Highness", Brave Hunter said cheerfully when he walked in to the room. He nodded to Pim, the owl and the elf with a smile. "Good day to you all." Then he sank into an armchair and said:

"Well what a day, it all worked out so beautifully!" Brave Hunter chuckled: "They were so busy partying, that we could sneak away unnoticed." He bobbed his head, while he took a glass of lemonade, took a sip of the delicious drink and licked his lips. Then he looked at the others in amusement and continued:

"At first it was quite scary. Just at the moment that the water had been replaced with the Bubbly Azules Shake, we saw a large group of giants coming our way."

Brave Hunter took another gulp before he continued speaking.

"It seems that one of the giants had not returned home last night." Pim jumped up from his armchair.

"That must be Bram!", he said in surprise. Brave Hunter looked at Pim in astonishment.

"Indeed, I believe that is the name they mentioned. How do you know that?" Pim wagged his tail and explained:

"Alice found him in the gorge."

"Alice?", asked Brave Hunter startled. "She was supposed to stay in the palace!" He looked quizzically at Pim. "And what do you mean by 'found'?", he continued shocked. The owl puffed his chest out and replied :

"A: she did not listen to you but went on the

road by herself. And B: Bram was lying with a sprained ankle in the gorge and Alice went to search for help." The dwarf nodded in agreement:

"Indeed, our doctor has bandaged Bram's ankle and ten of our strongest elves went along to roll two tree trunks to him. The doctor had decided then and there to take Bram with them, so he couldn't tell anyone that we were breaking down the dam."

With a loud thud the king smacked his glass down on the table. The others were startled by the noise.

"Yes", he growled, "and now all of Giant County knows of our plan." He was about to tell of the visit of the three giants when the door blew open and Alice flew in.

"Hi everybody", she said with a smiling face, "I am happy to see you all together." Brave Hunter dashed up and roared:

"You never should have left Kobold County by yourself." In a fright Alice flew up to the ceiling and whispered in a timid voice.

"I was just looking for you." Brave Hunter gestured at her to come down.

"I am not angry, just very worried. Who knows what could have happened! Please promise me that you will never ever do a thing like that again." Alice flew down and said in a soft voice:

"I promise, Brave Hunter." Brave Hunter made a friendly face and said in a fatherly way:

"That is good to hear". Alice nodded that she understood. Brave Hunter rubbed his hands and continued: "Please, tell us why you were so excited when you flew in?" Alice's face cleared up and she looked around:

"I have fantastic news!" And in detail she told them about her meeting with the father, uncle and brother of Bram. Everybody in the room was listening attentively.

When Alice was done with her story it was very quiet in the room. They all looked at each other in amazed surprise. Finally the owl broke the silence:

"A meeting with the king of the giants?", he said bewildered.

"Who knows, this might be a trap?", reacted the elf fiercely. Alice shook her little head and said decisively:

"I don't think that this is a trap. His uncle seemed to me to be a good hearted giant."

"Hmm", Brave Hunter said. "I heard Yuri and his Uncle Jan talking while we were hiding in the bushes. I too have the impression that this Uncle Jan has good intentions. Besides", he continued while the others were looking intensely at him, "I don't think we have any another choice." The kobold king nodded and chewed on his lip.

"Yes, I think we have to go. Do you all agree?" He looked inquisitively at the others. The elf straightened his pointy cap.

"If you are convinced that this is not a trap, then off course we have to go."

"There is no harm in finding out what they want", the owl put in.

So a little before seven o'clock the delegation of the F.J.E. Council and Brave Hunter were standing at the bridge. The kobold king stared into the distance and sighed:

"Still not a giant to be seen." The elf looked at his watch.

"It is not seven o' clock yet." The owl who was hovering high in the air, suddenly snapped:

"I see something coming." Now the others felt the earth trembling under their feet.

And not for long there were four giants standing before them; the giant king, Uncle Jan, Bram's father and another giant who looked very important.

"Good evening", the giant king greeted them.

"Good evening", the others reacted in unison.

"Lets us sit down, so we can see each other better", the king gestured.

When the giants were sitting in the high grass, Jan started to talk.

"I have explained to the king that you have changed the water into the Bubbly Azules Shake." The giant king nodded approving and said with a big smile:

"Good job, I really would like to hear how you have done that." Jan waved his hand and continued:

"I also told him that you wanted to sabotage the dam, because you could not meet our demands." Now the king made an angry face and roared while he stuck his finger in the air:

"I didn't think that was nice at all!" Jan looked at the king in irritation and continued again:

"We have discussed how to solve this problem." Now the kobold-king straightened his back and chuckled while holding his hand in front of his mouth.

"This, I like again." Jan swallowed and looked seriously at the others.

"The king is prepared to provide you with water if you bring him the Snake of Wisdom."

An awkward silence followed and everybody looked in a daze at Jan.

"The Snake of Wisdom?" Brave Hunter eventually asked in wonder. "I have never heard about it! What sort of snake is it?" Jan sucked some air through his teeth and explained:

"If you look straight into the eyes of the snake you will be filled with wise thoughts. Our king wants to possess this snake, so he will be wiser then anybody else and thus mightier." Brave Hunter scratched the back of his head.

"Hmm, and where can we find this snake?"

The kobold king who hadn't said anything so far, clicked his lips. His face was tight and tense and he looked fiercely at Jan.

"I assume that you are aware that no one ever came back from the search for the Snake of Wisdom?", he said irritated. Jan nodded and agreed:

"It is indeed not an easy task, but that is the demand of our king in exchange for water." The giant king stood up and roared with a loud voice:

"If you can change water in a delicious shake, you should be also able to bring me the snake." Bram's father put on an encouraging face and said hastily:

"During your search we won't close off the dam, so everybody will have enough water." The others were standing in a daze and nobody said a word.

When the giants were long and wel gone Pim broke the silence.

"Well, here we are, with an impossible task." The elf clenched his fist.

"I knew there had to be a catch!!", he said fiercely.

"They know very well that we can never deliver", snapped the owl.

"I have no idea what to do now", said the kobold king in despair. His face looked tired. Brave Hunter looked at the kobold king and asked:

"Why is it so difficult to find the Snake of Wisdom?"

The king sighed deeply, his eyes looked dull, he bit on his under lip and then started to tell:

"The Snake of Wisdom lives in the Third Dondragon. This is very deep under the earth. To get there you have to cross wild underground rivers, which all meet in a swirling waterfall. Then you have to cross a bed of spiders and maggots. If you survive this, you will reach an area strewn with hidden traps. If you step on one of these traps, you end up in an underground dungeon, from where you can never escape.

The story goes that there are giant spiders. If you manage not to fall into a trap and are able to follow the path, you reach a gate. Behind this gate lives the Snake of Wisdom. This gate is guarded by a three headed fire spitting dragon." The king looked dejectedly at Brave Hunter.

"And then off course it remains to be seen if the snake will come with you."

"Already many have tried to visit the Snake of Wisdom", added Pim. "But nobody has ever returned. That is why we are not really sure what to expect under there. It might be even worse than this." The elf drooped his shoulders.

"One thing is sure! Nobody ever came back from there. Game over!", he said sadly. "We will have to keep on working for the giants until eternity."

The king stood up and clapped his hands:
"I suggest that tomorrow morning we all get together. May be after a good night's sleep we might have a different outlook on things." The owl stretched his wings and yawned:
"Yes indeed, I am deadly tired. It has been such a busy day."

"At eight o'clock in the palace?", asked the elf. The king nodded.
"Eight o'clock is fine. OK, we will see each other then." And so everyone went to their beds exhausted.

THE DECISION.

Brave Hunter, Neston, Alice and Norma were sitting at the breakfast table.

"Wow, a Snake of Wisdom, that would be cool if we could meet him", Alice said enthusiastically. Brave Hunter had just told them about the assignments the giants had given them.

"We are going to help them of course hey, Brave Hunter?", asked Neston.

"Yes", sided Norma him, "after all we can fly over the swirling water and the bed of spiders and maggots." Enthusiastically Neston jumped from his chair.

"Yes, and all together we can handle the three headed dragon." He was striking wildly around him as if he was in a sword fight.

Brave Hunter shook his head smiling and shuffled his chair backwards.

"You sure are a bunch of daredevils!" Then he continued more seriously: "But you forget one thing, I can't fly." Norma bounced up.

"But I can take you with me on my broom!", she said spontaneously. Brave Hunter looked at her in surprise.

"Yes", Norma continued quickly," my broom can carry one extra person." Brave Hunter frowned.

"I can not bring you into danger", he said in a clear voice.

"But we have to help the kobolds, elves and animals, right?", Norma said in a decisive tone. "What good is it to have magic powers if you don't do the right thing with them?" Brave Hunter looked at the aggrieved expression on Norma's face.

"You can give help without putting yourself into danger", he reflected back. Norma put her forefinger in the air and said in a high pitched voice:

"Indeed, but I don't walk away from things when they become dangerous."

"She is quite right, Brave Hunter", Neston said excitedly, "we've got to help them."

"Yes, we can not just leave now", Alice chipped in.

Brave Hunter sighed deeply.

"So you are all quite sure that you want to go to the Third Dondragon?", he asked sternly.

"Off course!", all three shouted out together. Brave Hunter looked around, smiled and tapped his hands on the table.

"Ok, you have convinced me. We are going to search for this important snake."

"Yippee!!", they said joyfully in chorus and danced around the table. Brave Hunter had to laugh; he shuffled his chair backwards and stood up.

"Then I will go to the F.J.E. Council to tell them that we will search for the snake."

When Brave Hunter entered the meeting room the other members were already present.

"Good morning", Brave Hunter said cheerfully. "Did you all have a good night's sleep?" He looked smiling at the others and chuckled:

"Reading your faces I can tell that it's not the case." He dropped into a green armchair and slapped his hand on his knee.

"But", he started in a mischievous tone, "I have something to announce." The others looked at each other in surprise. Brave Hunter coughed a little.

"We have decided", he said, while gesturing with his hands, "and by we I mean: myself, Neston, Alice and Norma; to get the Snake of Wisdom for you."

They were all speechless. You could hear a pin drop as they looked at him with large wide eyes. The kobold king sat on the edge of his chair.

"No one ever came back from there", he said in a worried voice.

"We can fly, that is in our advantage", Brave Hunter replied.

"And how do you think you want to beat the dragon?", the owl wanted to know. Brave

Hunter shrugged his shoulders and pushed his lips together.

"We have to come up with a scheme." He looked around the room. "You sure don't want to work for the giants for ever, do you?" The others shook their heads. "And", he continued, "as I said before, we can fly. That can make all the difference."

Again, there was silence in the room. The faces were less gloomy now and you could see them thinking:

"Could this be possible?" Brave Hunter looked at the hopeful faces in front of him and continued cheerfully:

"Besides, I am curious about this snake. I would like to hear its wisdom!"

"It is worth a try", the elf reacted.

"I think it is a great offer!", screeched the owl. Suddenly the king bounced up from his throne, his crown slipping backwards on his head.

"If this is really what you want to do, we are off course very grateful." Brave Hunter nodded and answered in a deep voice:

"I have discussed this in detail with the others and they all insist that we do this." He made a little face to the others. "Believe me, I have no choice!"

"When do you want to leave?", asked the king.

"This morning, as soon as possible." The king nodded approving, gestured to a footman who was standing near the door and asked:

"Can you fetch Lauren?"

"Off course your majesty", he answered. He turned around and left the room. The king looked at Brave Hunter and explained:

"Lauren will take you to the well, which you have to descend."

The owl, Pim and the elf were chatting in excitement. The sadness they had felt this morning had evaporated.

"No-one has ever spoken with the Snake of Wisdom!" Brave Hunter heard the owl shrieking.

"It would be great if Brave Hunter could bring the snake back", he honked. The elf shook his head fiercely. The ball on his cap was bouncing back and forward.

"Yes, that would be a great idea. He can live in one of our mushroom houses. There is always a place for such an important person. And we will immediately make him a member of this council."

The elf looked roguishly around. The owl stretched his wings and puffed his chest out.

"The snake is off course going to live with us

in the forest", he said severely to the elf. "After all it is a snake and they belong in the forest and not in some sort of elf mushroom house. Besides....", the owl said haughtily," ......I am much better company for him." The elf bounced up angrily.

"What is wrong with our houses?" He looked furiously at the owl. "I can't imagine that the snake wants to put up with such a bighead as you", he hissed at the owl. Now it was the owl's turn to bounce up in anger.

"Bighead? Who are you calling bighead?", he yelled outraged, while fluttering his wings. With shiny furious eyes the elf and the owl looked at each other.

Pim who had been observing the situation from a distance, jumped up. He put his paws in the air and said in a loud voice:

"Quiet, both of you!" He looked severely at each of them in turn and asked in astonishment:

"What is this all about? Brave Hunter and his friends risk their lives to go to the third Dondragon and you two are argueing about such trivial stuff?" Pim shook his head in disgust. "I really don't get it. But one thing I know for sure", he said pointing at them "you two still have a lot to learn!" He looked straight into the eyes of the owl and the elf.

For a little while it was very quiet in the

room. The owl and the elf threw each other shameful glances.

"You are right", squeaked the owl to Pim. He spread his right wing towards to the elf and said with in a small voice:

"I am sorry that I criticised your mushroom houses. I really didn't mean it." The elf shook the wing of the owl and said softly:

"I am sorry that I called you a bighead. I actually think that you are very clever." Pim smiled and thought:

"The Snake of Wisdom would be very pleased!"

Brave Hunter got up.

"I am going to get my rucksack, because we need to pack some food for the journey". The king also stood up and walked with him to the door.

"Ask our cook to pack something delicious." Brave Hunter closed the door behind him and walked to the kitchen.

"Good morning, master cook!", he called out cheerfully to the kobold with the big white cap. The cook waved joyfully with his wooden spoon.

"I have already got the message. I am preparing lunch for you and your fellow travellers." Brave Hunter looked surprised and chuckled:

"Well, news is really travelling as fast as lightning around here." The cook grinned back:

"And they expect me to work at that speed as well!"

Then Brave Hunter walked to the breakfast room, where Neston, Alice and Norma were still chatting away. Neston who was facing the door saw Brave Hunter coming in.

"And how did they react?", he asked in anticipation. Norma and Alice turned around abruptly. Brave Hunter strode towards the table and looked seriously at the others:

"Eventually they found it a good idea." Neston jumped up from his chair in joy.

"So, today we are going to the Third Dondragon?" Brave Hunter smiled at Neston's enthusiastic reaction and nodded in agreement:

"They are looking for Lauren to take us to the well that leads to the Third Dondragon." He had a knowing look on his face.

"He may arrive at any moment and then I want to leave immediately. I suggest that you get ready for the trip. Put on some warm clothes, because it will be cold so deep under the ground."

All three got up and walked to their rooms. Brave Hunter followed to put something warmer on as well.

THE THIRD DONDRAGON.

"The well is behind the bushes." Lauren pointed forward with his finger. First Lauren had taken them through a maze of underground corridors. Then they had climbed up a rope ladder. And now they had been walking for about half an hour above the ground. They were in a valley that was surrounded by high mountains. The sun could hardly reach her beams into the valley. It was cold. A sparse scattering of bushes and small trees surrounded them.

Despite the lack of sunshine in the valley, Neston had trouble with the light. After being underground for a while, his eyes took some time getting accustomed to the brightness. So when Lauren was pointing his finger forwards, Neston really had to squeeze his eyes together to see properly.

"You mean over there?", he asked, while he pointed to a group of bushes. Lauren nodded. Neston gave him a sideways glance.

"I am going to beat you!", he yelled teasing at Lauren and sprinted forward. Immediately Lauren set off and together they reached the well gasping for breath.

"You are faster then I thought", panted Neston.

"What do you think?", chuckled Lauren. "The times I had to run fast, to be at home in time, are countless!"

The well, which was surrounded by bushes, was made of clay. Above the well was a shelter made of reed. Neston hung over the edge of the well.

"It looks deep and dark", he said to Lauren while he shivered. He cupped hands around his mouth and yelled into the well:

"Echo, echo!" But no noise came back. Neston looked in surprise at Lauren and called out again.

"Echo, echo!" But still no noise was reflected.

"Who on earth are you calling?", Alice asked curiously. She had just arrived with Brave Hunter and Norma.

"I am trying to find out how deep the well is", Neston answered her.

"And you want to ask Echo? Who is he?", said Alice laughing. Neston shook his head, threw a meaningful glance at Lauren and mumbled:

"Girls!"

Brave Hunter had put his rucksack against the wall of the well.

"No Alice, echo is not a person or an animal, but just a word", answered Brave Hunter instead of Neston.

"When Neston's voice reaches the bottom of the well it will bounce back. Just like when you shout near mountains or in caves. That sound reflection is called an 'echo'." Alice looked puzzled at Brave Hunter and said in wonder:

"But Neston's voice didn't come back at all!" Brave Hunter nodded.

"Yes, I noticed that too. This might mean that the well is very, very deep."

He bent down and took a little rock from the ground.

"Lets us see, if we can hear this rock hit the floor", Brave Hunter said to the others. With a swing he threw the rock into the well. Everybody was hanging with his or her ear above the well, to listen to the stone hit the bottom. Neston pulled a doubtful face and shook his head.

"Nothing to be heard, nothing at all." Norma also shook her head.

"I didn't hear anything either." Brave Hunter rubbed his hands and said cheerfully:

"Well guys, this means we have to go way down."

"I am not a guy", Alice responded.

"Ok, boy, fairy and witch girl, it means we have to go very deep. Is this all right with you Alice?", he winked. Alice made a face.

"Oh look, here is the ladder!", Neston called out enthusiastically, while he pulled on the bars of the ladder.

"Yep!", said Lauren while he went sitting on the well.

"With this ladder you can go all the way down. I will wait for you here. Be sure you come back in one piece hey?", he said worried. Brave Hunter sat himself on the well and swung his legs over the edge. He took the ladder in his hands and lowered himself down. While he stood on the ladder he looked at Alice.

"I assume that you will fly down?" Alice nodded.

"Yes I will use my wings." Then he looked inquisitively at Norma. She was standing leaning on her broom and shook her head.

"No, the well is too narrow to use the broom." Then she waved her arms and a cloud appeared around the broom. When it cleared Norma was holding a small broom of the size of a pencil. She put the broom in the pocket of her skirt and sat on the well. Brave Hunter gestured at Norma.

"You go after me." Then he turned his head to Neston.

"You descend after Norma." He turned to Alice.

"You will be last. If anything should happen to the ladder you can always fly up quickly." He looked around and asked in a low voice:

"Understood?"

"Loud and clear", all three answered in unison. Brave Hunter held the ladder tight and lowered him-self.

"Well Alice, now it is your turn", said Lauren when Neston's head had disappeared into the well. Alice nodded nervously at him.

"I do find it a little bit creepy", she whispered. "It looks so dark and deep." She shivered a bit. Lauren had a worried look on his face.

"If you find it too scary, you should not go, you know." Decisively Alice shook her little head.

"No, I will go down." She smiled shyly at Lauren and then flew into the well.

"See you tonight!" she heard Lauren calling after her.

It was dark in the well. Brave Hunter had given Alice a small flashlight. She held it in her hand and shone it on the wall. Gradually her eyes got used to the dark. A little further down she saw Neston's head. When she was near him she remarked:

"We have gone down quite deep already." Neston blew some air through his lips.

"Indeed, it is quite a climb."

"You are almost there!", they heard Brave Hunter call out to them. Alice shone her flashlight down and saw Brave Hunter and Norma standing, looking up. She flew past Neston and landed on the stony ground.

Not much later Neston stood next to her, shivering.

"Well, it is dark and cold!" Norma handed everybody a flashlight. In the distance they heard water swirling.

"It sounds as if we have to go that way", Brave Hunter pointed towards the noise of the swirling water and started to walk in that direction. The others followed him. Soon they felt water drops on their faces. Further down they saw glow worms, on the walls. The blue light, which they radiated, gave it all a magical atmosphere.

The swirling of the water was getting louder and louder. When they walked around the bend they saw a big savage river. The high waves were pounding on rocks in the stream. Foam splashed around. It was really a frightening sight. Brave Hunter put up his hand indicating they should stop.

"I think from here we have to fly," he called out above the noise of the raging river. He took his rucksack and put all the lanterns in it, except Alice's because she was flying with her wings and didn't need her hands. Then he took out the case from his rucksack and sprinkled

Neston with the magic powder. In a couple of seconds Neston was just as small as Alice. Then Brave Hunter took out a stick from his rucksack and handed it over to Neston. It was the magic flying stick that Neston was given by a fairy in Jingleland.

Neston held the stick with both hands. He flew up a bit and somersaulted in the air.

"Yippee, I can still do it!", he said relieved to the others. Norma whizzed her broom back to a normal size. She gestured at Brave Hunter, while throwing her right leg over the broom.

"It is the easiest, if you sit in front of me", she said to Brave Hunter, when he stood next to her. He nodded in agreement and climbed on the broom, held it tight with both hands and mumbled to himself:

"This has to work!" Then he looked at the others, and yelled above the roaring water:

"Try to fly as high as possible to avoid the splashing waves. We will wait for each other at the waterfall."

"Good luck to you all!"

Norma pointed the broom up and off they went into the air. The broom swayed a bit at first because of the weight but after a few seconds it balanced and flew smoothly. Alice was flying just behind them and Neston was last. Just before they crossed the water Norma

climbed up a bit higher and then they flew over the swirling, wild river. The splashing water made so much noise that they couldn't talk with one and another. Water drops flew around their ears.

The river was flowing in a series of peculiar bends. Norma, Neston and Alice had to navigate very well in order not to fly into the rocky walls. Those walls were getting greyer and greyer. At a certain stage they even turned black. After three quarters of an hour flying they saw the river drop down into a very steep waterfall. They flew over the waterfall. Carefully Norma landed her broom on the path that lay just behind it.

"Phew, that was quite a wild ride", Alice sighed as she landed softly next to Norma. She saw Neston flying over the waterfall. He held his stick tight. With a big grin he landed next to the others and said excitedly:

"Wow, that was really cool!"

Brave Hunter got off the broom and sprinkled Neston with the magic powder, in order to get him back to his normal size. Then he started to walk along the path. The others followed him.

"We really have to watch out for the area with maggots, snakes and spiders", he warned the others. He stared into the distance. The path was quite winding. Carefully they kept on walking. Alice was shining her lantern from left to right.

"What a gloomy place it is", she whispered to Norma. Norma nodded tensely, while squinting her eyes and staring into the darkness. In the meantime Neston had passed Brave Hunter and walked in front of the others. He looked back.

"Come on you guys, what are you waiting for?", he called out impatiently.

"Not too fast, Neston!", Brave Hunter warned him. But Neston didn't listen and went around the bend. Brave Hunter shook his head and kept on walking.

THE GIANT SPIDERS.

When they had taken the bend as well, they didn't see Neston there.

"Where did he go?", asked Alice in surprise. Quickly Brave Hunter took the next bend. He shook his head.

"No, he isn't here either", he said while turning around. Then he looked at Norma in shock and asked in alarm:

"Where did Alice go?" Norma looked behind her in disbelief and then stared at Brave Hunter with big eyes.

"She was standing next to me just a second ago", she shrieked.

Brave Hunter had a concerned frown on his face and sighed deeply.

"Hmm, first Neston and now Alice." Suddenly Norma held her forefinger to her mouth.

"Shh, I hear something." Brave Hunter pricked his ears.

"It seems as if Neston is calling from behind these black walls", he mumbled softly to Norma.

"Help us, we are trapped!", they heard more clearly.

Suddenly a long hairy arm reached out from

the wall. The arm tried to grab Norma who screamed out loudly. In a flash the arm disappeared back into the wall. Norma rubbed her sweaty forehead with the back of her hand and said with a trembling voice:

"That gave me a fright! Fortunately I am wearing my medallion." (*See Brave Hunter and the Witches. This medallion protects her from evil. She got this from her father the Mighty Sorcerer of the High Mountains, when she was just a baby. When she is really in danger, she can make a wish by rubbing the medallion.*)

Brave Hunter looked from the wall to Norma and from Norma to the wall.

"Off course, the medallion you got from your father. It protects you against evil." Brave Hunter frowned and continued pondering:

"Well, we know how Neston and Alice disappeared."

Norma walked over to the wall where the hairy arm had disappeared. She rubbed her hand over the rocky surface.

"Strange, there is no opening to be found." She continued touching the wall with her hand and felt a smooth stone. She pushed it slightly and slowly the ground under their feet moved away. They slid down a sort of slippery ramp and before they could react they were in a round chamber and the ground above their heads was closing again. In surprise they looked at each other. The room was dry and warm. The walls were covered with large spider webs. In front of them they saw a large heavy wooden door.

Brave Hunter walked to the door and put his ear against it. He shook his head.

"Nothing to be heard", he said softly to Norma. Carefully he pushed the handle down and opened the door. They were standing in a large round room. Several bundles were dangling from the ceiling. They looked like mummies wrapped in spider webs.

"What is this all about?", asked Norma in surprise, pointing at the bundles. One of them started to swing and suddenly they heard Neston's voice.

"Brave Hunter, Norma? Are you there?", they heard him asking.

Norma walked towards the bundle and asked tensely:

"Are you in there Neston?" Again, it swung back and forward.

"Yes", they heard Neston saying in a small voice.

"A giant spider grabbed me and spun a web around me."

"Is Alice hanging here too?", asked Brave Hunter looking around him.

"I am hanging here, Brave Hunter!" A thin

voice was coming from the right. Now they saw a small bundle swinging from the ceiling. Brave Hunter clenched his fist.

"We are going to free you immediately, my friends!" He was reaching towards the ceiling to take down the bundles, when the door swung open. Two giant spiders stood there. They were enormous with huge lumpy abdomens. Their hairy legs were as thick as cables. Big black antennas sprouted from their heads and wobbled back and forth. Their eyes looked like luminous saucers and rolled around the room surveying the scene. Their heads were dominated by a large mouth, filled with razor-sharp teeth and long slimy tongues that popped in and out as they licked their lips.

One of the spiders pointed at Brave Hunter and Norma.

"Hey, here are the two other dishes, he said enthusiastically to the other spider, who nodded while still licking his lips.

"Yes, and we didn't even have to catch them", he chuckled evilly, while nodding to Brave Hunter.

The fat one seems like an especially nice snack." He stuck out his long foreleg to grab Brave Hunter, but he warded it off easily with a karate strike.

"Ok then, we'll start with the smaller dish", the spider smacked his lips, while pointing at

Norma but she was already rubbing her medallion fiercely. Before the spider could move forward the two spiders were frozen in place, standing like a statue.

Brave Hunter looked approvingly at Norma.

"Well done, witchy. But now we have to hurry, because the spell doesn't work for long." Quickly Brave Hunter took down the two bundles from the ceiling. Norma took the small one and Brave Hunter the big one and both started to unroll them as fast as they could. The bundles were spinning around like tops. After a few seconds Neston's face appeared. He was as red as a beetroot.

"Phew, am I happy to see you", he said in relief. Once Alice was unwrapped, she fluttered her wings and sighed:

"It felt very closed in." Brave Hunter gestured anxiously.

"Come on! We have to get out of here quickly. Soon the spiders will come back to life." Neston pointed at the door and said in fright:

"But we can't get out of here. The spiders are blocking the door. And there is no other way out."

Brave Hunter looked at Norma and then to the others.

"Hang on tight to Norma! Norma, rub the

medallion and wish us back to the place where we were before", he said in a hurry. Quickly Neston and Alice grabbed Norma's arm. Brave Hunter also held on tight while she rubbed her medallion. Alice squeezed her eyes tightly together. She found the situation really scary. For a minute she peeped through her eyelashes at the door. She saw some life coming back into the spiders.

"Quick Norma, wish us back up!", she screamed in fright, while pulling Norma's sleeve. Again she squeezed her eyes tight and then she felt a gust of wind.

When she opened her eyes, they were back at the waterfall.

Brave Hunter took out his little case.

"We have to get out of here as soon as possible, before the spiders find out where we are. We will continue flying." Quickly he put some magic powder on Neston's hair. Meanwhile Norma got her broom ready and Brave Hunter jumped on it. In a flash all four were in the air and flew as swiftly as possible over the path.

"Hurry, we have to get out of the area to where their long arms can't reach", Brave Hunter yelled over his shoulder to the others. Alice held tight to the broom while fluttering her wings. They had almost passed the notorious bend.

"Hold on we are almost there", Brave Hunter panted, "then they can't reach us anymore."

"Help!", Neston suddenly yelled. A spidery arm was coming from the wall and tried to grab him. Holding tight to his flying stick he dived down sharply. The arm missed. But the spider didn't give up. Again it tried to grab Neston. But luckily Neston was just too fast for the hairy creature. He shot up like an arrow.

"Quick Neston, around the bend!", Brave Hunter yelled. Neston zigzagged through the air. Another near miss as an arm shot out. Neston had big drops of sweat sliding from his forehead. He manoeuvred his flying stick forward and in a few seconds he was safe and sound around the corner.

The others had dropped their speed and now hung quietly in the air.

"Phew, that was close, Neston", said Alice with a hoarse voice. Neston rubbed away the sweat from his forehead.

"Indeed it was very scary. I had no intention of being wrapped up like a mummy again", he said a little dazed. But then a grin appeared on his face.

"I sure was way too fast for him, hey? Brady should have seen this." (*Brady is a fairy from Jingleland. Neston got his flying stick from Brady's sister.*) I think he never would have guessed how I could fly with this thing."

"My compliments, Neston", Norma smiled, "your flying ability is unbeatable."

"Indeed, a masterly example of aerial agility", Brave Hunter agreed. Neston smiled from ear to ear. Quietly the group flew further down the path.

"I wonder where the bed with spiders and maggots is", Alice sounded worried.

"I was never keen on spiders and now I have been wrapped up by one, I have become quite scared." Brave Hunter thought for a while and said hesitantly:

"I have no idea. I had expected them by now. Maybe there is no such thing."

"I hope not", Alice sighed.

The path continued on its windy way. The group zigzagged along it

"Have you ever seen a dragon?", Neston suddenly asked Alice. She shook her little head.

"No, but I do know that they are very dangerous creatures. They spit fire through their nostrils. They have a very long tongue with which they can gulp you down and their teeth are as sharp as knives." She shivered. Neston looked inquisitive and said:

"Don't you worry, I am going to beat the dragon!" Norma, who had been following the conversation, shook her head and laughed.

"That I want to see!"

JARO, THE CHILD DRAGON.

While Brave Hunter, Neston, Alice and Norma were flying further down the path, the dragon was standing in front of a blue iron fence. He played a dragon's game. He had a stone which was attached to a piece of long elastic. One end of the elastic was anchored tightly to the ground. The dragon had the stone in one claw and he hit it with his other claw. The stone flew forward and at the same moment the dragon spat fire from his nostrils. When the stone was at the end of the elastic, it bounced back and the dragon caught it. He studied the stone with his big dragon eyes.

"Hmm, missed again!", mumbled Jaro, which was his name. "I will never learn it!"

The purpose of the game was to hit the stone with the fire from his nostrils. The fire had to shrivel up the stone. The better you aimed, the hotter the fire would be, and the faster the stone would shrivel. His brother Daro was very good at the game. Within three attempts he could shrivel the stone. Jaro never succeeded no matter how many times he tried. Jaro was practising hard because he wanted to beat his brother someday.

Jaro lived with his father, mother, brother

Daro and sister Dana in Dragon village. The Dragon village was just behind the fort of the Snake of Wisdom. It was the duty of the dragons to protect the Snake of Wisdom. They had been doing this as long as his grandpa could remember. And that was very long ago, because his grandpa was really old - *850* years. Jaro was only *60* years old. This was the first year that he went to dragonschool. His brother Daro was much bigger, he was *120* years old and went to dragonhighschool. And his sister Dana, who was only *40* years old, was still in dragonkindergarten. When a dragon turned 60, they had to help with guarding the fort for the Snake of Wisdom.

This was only the third time Jaro had the post. Jaro looked around bored. Posting days always lasted so endlessly long. Nothing ever happened.

"I don't understand why we have to guard here. Nothing ever happens!", he roared to himself. He hit another stone and spat some fire. Suddenly he heard a noise in the distance. He pricked his ears up and stared into the distance. But it was dead quiet again. Jaro shook his large head which was covered with bumps.

"I must have imagined it!" He looked around for a few moments longer and then started to hit the rock again.

But Jaro had not imagined it. The noise he had heard was the laughter and chatting of Neston, Alice and Norma. Immediately Brave Hunter had ordered them to be quiet.

"Silence, we are getting closer to the Snake of Wisdom. The dragon might be able to hear us now." Promptly everybody hushed up, not feeling too secure. Norma leaned over her broom and tilted her head sideways.

"I believe I hear somebody spitting fire. Do you hear it too?" she asked Brave Hunter softly. He closed his eyes and listened tensely. Then he nodded to Norma.

"I thing you are right." He gestured to Neston and Alice so stay behind them. Alice didn't need to be told twice. Neston hesitated a second, but the stern look on Brave Hunter's face made him change his mind rapidly.

They kept on flying cautiously. And then when they had turned another corner, they saw a big lake with an island in the middle. And in the middle of the island was a bunker made of blue stone. The island itself was surrounded by a big blue iron fence. The fence looked beautiful with all kinds of decorations of animals, plants and flowers. In the middle of the fence was a big gate, decorated with copper designs. Behind the gate was an alley leading to the bunker. Before the gate they saw Jaro standing.

"The dragon!", Alice whispered in fright.

"Sshh", Neston held his forefinger to his lips. Alice understood immediately and didn't say another word. Softly Brave Hunter gave Norma a tap on the shoulder and whispered:

"Please, take your medallion and wish the dragon into stone." Norma got her medallion from under her blouse and rubbed it forcefully.

"I wish that the dragon was made of stone", she whispered softly. Tentatively the others watched to see if the dragon turned into stone. But there was no sign of any change.

The dragon threw a rock into the air and blew fire on it.

"It seems to me as if he is playing a game", Neston said astonished. Brave Hunter shook his head in surprise.

"It doesn't seem to work, Norma, nothing happens. Which makes sense because you are not in danger." Brave Hunter scratched an ear and said:

"If you give me the medallion, I will walk towards the dragon. Once it sees me, I will be in danger and then I will wish him into stone." Norma hesitated a bit.

"I don't mind doing it myself." Brave Hunter shook his head.

"Out of the question, I don't want to put you into danger! I am going and nobody else." Norma lifted the chain of the medallion over her head and put it in Brave Hunter's hand. He held the medallion tightly in his fist. He looked at everybody with a penetrating glance.

"You all stay here until I call you", he said in a stern voice. Then he turned around and walked to the lake.

Unaware, Jaro was throwing another stone. He didn't see Brave Hunter approaching at all. A flash of fire came out of his nostrils. Brave Hunter was now standing on the edge of the lake. He was more than close enough for the dragon, to see him.

"It's quite a big animal", he thought a little bit frightened. Then he took a deep breath and shouted at the top of his voice:

"Dragon, I am here!" Jaro turned around in a daze and looked at Brave Hunter in amazement. He had never seen a human before. He tilted his head to the left and asked in surprise:

"Who are you and what are you doing here?"

With all his strength Brave Hunter rubbed the medallion, while he murmured:

"Dragon, be stone. Dragon turn into stone." But Jaro remained alive and kicking and looked at Brave Hunter with big doggy eyes. He stuck his neck forward, blinked and asked kindly:

"You sure look funny, all fireballs in the air!

What is your name?"

Brave Hunter was speechless. He had prepared himself for the worst. He had thought that the moment the dragon saw him, he would be roaring and growling, stamping towards him, and trying to fry him alive. But nothing of the sort was happening. The dragon looked at him with big surprised eyes, even asking for his name! Brave Hunter looked down at the medallion.

"That is why it is not working, I am not in danger!", he thought. He looked up again and saw Jaro still looking at him with big inquisitive eyes.

For a minute Brave Hunter could only blink his eyes but then said in a clear, loud voice:

"I am a human and my name is Brave Hunter. What is your name?" Jaro gave a small bow.

"My name is Jaro and I am a dragon child. Today it is my turn to guard the Snake of Wisdom." He pointed to the gate with his claw. There was a moments silence. Then Jaro asked:

"What are you doing here, Brave Hunter?"

"I, uh, I, eh," Brave Hunter couldn't find the right words. "What would he say to Jaro? That he wanted to take the Snake of Wisdom with him?" He blew some air into his cheeks, so his

171

face ballooned up, then he left the air escape between his lips. He furrowed his eyebrows, then he looked straight into the dragon's eyes and said in a clear voice:

"I would like to meet the Snake of Wisdom."

Jaro had a puzzled look on his face. Finally he asked:

"And why do you want to speak to the Snake of Wisdom?"

"I want to talk to him about the giant king", Brave Hunter answered him. "The giant king wants to invite the Snake of Wisdom for a visit." Jaro shook his lumpy head.

"No, that is not possible", he responded immediately. "The Snake of Wisdom never appears above the ground."

"Never, ever?", Brave Hunter asked in surprise.

"If the Snake of Wisdom is exposed to day-light or even to moonlight it will shrivel. That is why the snake never goes up", Jaro explained calmly to Brave Hunter.

"I understand", nodded Brave Hunter. "But nevertheless could I speak with him?" Jaro loo-ked at Brave Hunter and said hesitantly:

"I will ask the Snake of Wisdom. Wait there just a minute, I will be right back." He turned around and disappeared through the gate.

After a little while the gate opened again and

Jaro appeared in the door opening. He smiled at Brave Hunter and waved his claws.

"The Snake of Wisdom will receive you." Brave Hunter looked relieved, but then threw a questioning look at the water in front of them.

"How do I cross the lake?" Jaro shrugged his shoulders and replied:

"I always swim across it. Just wait a tick, I will bring you over."

And before he had finished the last sentence Jaro had jumped into the water. In a couple of strokes he had reached the shore on the other side of the river.

"Just jump on my back and I will swim you across", he called to Brave Hunter. Brave Hunter hesitated for a second, but then threw his leg over Jaro's neck and sat on his shoulder.

"Are you comfortable?", he asked Brave Hunter, while looking back.

"Very comfortable thank you, high and dry", Brave Hunter answered cheerfully.

"Just hang on to my ears." And splash, Jaro jumped into the lake again.

THE SNAKE OF WISDOM

When they reached the island, Brave Hunter stepped from Jaro's shoulder, made a bow and laughed

"Thank you, your honourable dragon." Jaro grinned and pointed at the gate.

"You have to go through that door over there to get to the Snake of Wisdom." Brave Hunter nodded and walked to the gate. Carefully he pushed the handle down. The big heavy gate squeaked as it opened. Behind the gate was a corridor, which was lit by burning torches on the wall. Brave Hunter closed the gate behind him and walked in slowly. At the end of the corridor he saw a copper door.

"That must be the door that leads to the Snake of Wisdom", thought Brave Hunter with a pounding heart. He found it quite exciting to meet such an important creature. Softly he knocked on the door.

"Do come in, Brave Hunter", a hissing voice said. Brave Hunter pushed the door open and stepped into a round room. The room was sparsely lit with torches. On his right was a marble fountain, which was clearly lit by torches shining above it. On top of the fountain stood a marble snake, wrapped around the tree, while spitting water from his mouth. The noise of the splashing water filled the room. To the left was a table with three big bowls of glass on it. The bowls were filled with water and coloured scented oil. The sweet scent of lavender and jasmine filled the air. In the middle of the room was a large square marble pillar, with a thick dark green pillow. On this pillow lay the Snake of Wisdom. He had stretched his head far out and looked with penetrating eyes at Brave Hunter.

"Hmm, so you are Brave Hunter, a human, how interesting", hissed the snake calmly. "Come on in and take a seat on this couch." Feeling very out of place Brave Hunter shuffled into the area and sat down on the marble bench in front of the pillar. The snake stretched his neck even further and checked Brave Hunter from head to toe.

"So, you are a human", hissed the snake again. "I have never seen a human this close. What is a human doing in the land of giants and kobolds?" The snake pulled his neck back and curled up on his pillow and continued kindly:

"And what brings you to me?" Brave Hunter folded his hands, put them in his lap and said softly:

"That is quite a long story." The snake twisted a bit and hissed calmly:

That doesn't matter, I love hearing stories."

Brave Hunter coughed a little bit and then started to tell about the letter he had received from Corsica. He described in detail how the witches had been chased out of Jingleland. He recounted the meeting of the kobolds and the giants. And finally he told about the giant's king request to bring him the Snake of Wisdom.

When Brave Hunter finally had finished speaking, the Snake was silent at first. Eventually he hissed:

"That is quite a story, Brave Hunter. Quite a story." He shook his head and hissed:

"This giant king is really dumb and also terribly mean, keeping all the water for himself."

He twisted his long body and looked at Brave Hunter.

"Unfortunately, I cannot come with you, I can't tolerate either sun or moonlight. But I do want to help you." The snake pointed at the table with the glass bowls on it.

"Under the table is a basket, could you get that for me please?"

"Off course", answered Brave Hunter politely, while he got up to get the basket. He put the basket, made of reed, by his feet and sat on the bench again.

Please open the lid", hissed the snake at him.

Carefully Brave Hunter lifted the lid and saw that the basket was filled with all kinds of hand-mirrors. The mirrors were decorated with small marble snakes.

"Just take out a mirror", the snake ordered.

Brave Hunter took one out of the basket and closed the lid. The snake said with twinkling eyes:

"I see you thinking: why do I need a mirror?" He shook his head a bit and continued joyfully with hissing voice:

"Don't you worry, your hair is nicely combed." Brave Hunter grinned back:

"Thank you for the compliment. I can tell you are a connoisseur!"

The snake looked serious again and continued in an important tone:

"This is my gift to the king of the giants." Brave Hunter looked doubtfully at the snake, but the snake continued unperturbed:

"One who looks into the mirror will be confronted with his own dumbness. And the realisation of this dumbness will be the basis for wise thoughts."

Brave Hunter took his rucksack and put the mirror into it. Then he looked at the snake and said solemnly:

"In the name of the kobolds, gnomes and the

animals in the forest I want to thank you with all our heart. I hope the giant king will come to his senses."The snake's tongue slid out of its mouth as he hissed:

"That he will certainly do - the mirror never fails."

He twisted his body and then stretched up, to look Brave Hunter straight into the eyes:

"You seem to my like a good and wise person." He held Brave Hunter's gaze and continued:

"I wish you a safe journey back and will see to it that the giant spiders don't bother you this time, so you can return safely to the well." Brave Hunter got up and said in a warm voice to the snake, before he walked out of the door:

"Thank you very much for receiving me and for this mirror."

THE SNAKE'S GIFT

Brave Hunter sat in the kobold king's office. Brave Hunter, Neston, Norma and Alice had returned without any problems or obstacles. The kobold king sat behind his desk and leaned back in his leather chair.

"Hmm, and we have to hand over this mirror to the giant king?", said the kobold king in a questioning tone after Brave Hunter told the story.

The king took a bell from his desk and shook it. A footman appeared in the doorway.

"Can you take a message to the giant king to let him know that we will visit him tonight?"

"I will send someone straight away, your majesty", he said politely. The kobold king looked at Brave Hunter.

"Why don't you go freshen yourself up, before we go. I will send for you, when we depart." Brave Hunter shuffled his chair backwards, got up and said lightly:

"I sure could use a hot shower. See you tonight your majesty."

It was about half past seven, when a small group knocked on the giant king's palace door. The group consisted of: the delegation of the F.J.E Council, Brave Hunter, Lauren, Neston,

Alice and Norma. The doorman opened up and roared:

"You are expected, please come in."

They looked at each other in bewilderment. Phooey, that doorman was sure large and his voice tremendously loud. Neston held his hands to his ears. They walked through an enormous hallway. Our friend's eyes were popping out of their heads. The doors, which opened onto the hallway, were as high as trees and as wide as large rivers. The corridor was so wide that at least two horse drawn carriages could pass each other with ease. A massive chandelier hung from the ceiling and illuminated the hall.

The doorman walked in front of them with huge steps. Finally he stopped at a large wooden door. He knocked on the door with his enormous giant knuckles. The noise boomed down the hallway.

"Enter!", they heard a voice shouting. The doorman swung the door open and waved the group in. Shuffling they walked into the meeting room. At the large meeting table sat the five ministers, the three scholars, Bram, his father and the giant king. The giant king smiled and gestured to the group to approach.

"Come on in, come on in." He rubbed his hands and grinned:

"Quickly show me the snake, I can't wait."
Brave Hunter put up his hand and said
solemnly:

"Everything in its own time, your majesty."
Minister Jan gestured at them to sit down at
the meeting table. He looked at the group and
asked kindly. "What can we offer you to drink?"
They all felt like a glass of juice. Within
moments a footman appeared with a tray of
filled glasses.

Alice who sat next to Bram, asked softly:
"How is your ankle, Bram?" He whispered
back:

"Fine, I went to the doctor yesterday and he
told me that in six weeks I will be running like
the wind again." He gave Alice a sideways
glance and grinned:

"At the moment I am spoiled rotten by everybody." Alice grinned back:

"I am sure you have no problem with that!"

"Sh, ssssh", Bram's father muttered. The
king banged his hammer on the table and
demanded:

"Silence everybody! I want to hear what
Brave Hunter has to say. Did you find the
Snake of Wisdom?" With a tense expression on
his face he looked at Brave Hunter. All eyes
were now on Brave Hunter. It was dead quite in
the meeting room. You could hear a needle

drop. Brave Hunter looked around the table and started:

"Indeed, I found the Snake of Wisdom." Pleased, the giant king jumped up of his chair and yelled enthusiastically:

"Yippee, where is the snake?" But Jan gestured the king to sit down and said calmly:

"We should listen to what he has got to say, your majesty." Quickly the king sat back in his seat and nodded tensely at Brave Hunter.

Brave Hunter scratched his throat and resumed:

"Indeed, I have met the Snake of Wisdom. And I have told the snake about you, your majesty." He nodded at the giant king, who beamed and looked with pride around the table. Then Brave Hunter put his rucksack on the table and took out the hand-mirror. He looked at the giant king and said solemnly:

"This is the snake's gift to you."

He wanted to hand over the mirror to the king, but the king turned deep red in anger.

"What!!", he roared, "a mirror, a mirror! How dare you show up here and offer me a mirror?" The king jumped up and stamped around the boardroom.

"I want to have the Snake of Wisdom", he whined on. In the meantime the fat minister had taken the mirror out of Brave Hunter's

hand. He looked intensely at the mirror. He saw the marble frame and the marble handle, decorated with marble snakes.

When he looked in the mirror, he reacted in fright. The fat minister brought the mirror closer to his face and looked intensely at it. Then he pushed the mirror away from him. He frowned and shook his head in confusion. He wanted to bring the mirror closer again, but then the giant king grabbed the mirror out of his hands.

"What is there to see in the mirror?", he snapped. The fat minister looked confused and stared at the king with glassy eyes. The giant king shook his head in irritation and threw a glance at the mirror. The others saw that the king's eyes became as big as saucers.

"What is this!" What is this?", he muttered shocked. "This, this, this is not me!"

The king kept looking into the mirror as if hypnotised. They all were watching the confused king who kept on staring into the mirror. It was dead quiet in the room, the only sound you could hear was the ticking of the big standing clock. It seemed to last an eternity, but slowly the shocked expression on the king's face changed. His eyes became clearer, his jaw line sharper and a determined expression appeared around his mouth. Finally he put the mirror calmly on the meeting table and sat down again.

Peacefully he looked around the room and looked at everybody, one by one. Then he passed the mirror to the fat minister and said severely:

"Look into the mirror until I say that you can put it down." The fat minister was still confused and shocked about what he had seen just a minute ago. So he shook his head, because he never wanted to look into that mirror again! But the giant king didn't want to hear about it and ordered again:

"Look into the mirror!"

Slowly the fat minister took the mirror from the table and brought it to his face. His head was as red as a beetroot and his eyes were glazy and confused. But after a while the same thing that had happened with the giant king happened to him. The expression of his face changed, his usual colour returned and his eyes became clear and bright. When the giant king found that he had looked into the mirror long enough he said:

"Now pass the mirror to the next minister."

And in this way the mirror was passed around the table. From minister to minister, from scholar to scholar. When everybody had looked into the mirror, the giant king took it again and laid it down in front of him. The others looked seriously at him and waited on what he was going to say. The king put his hands down on the table and addressed Brave Hunter.

"I want to thank you very much for bringing me the gift of the Snake of Wisdom." Brave Hunter nodded back and took a stealthy look at Jan the minister.

"The mirror has worked", Brave Hunter thought relieved.

The giant king turned around to the kobold king and said:

"We", the giant king nodded in the direction of the ministers and the scholars. "We were greedy and wrong to ask so much from you." The giant king sighed and his eyes looked sad.

"I am really very, very sorry!" Then his eyes slid over the faces of the owl, the elf and the squirrel Pim.

"From now on you never have to pay for water again. You have paid enough for the rest of you lives."

The king threw a glance at the scholars.

"We will manage the water in such a manner to ensure that there will be enough for everybody all year round." All the ministers and scholars nodded heavily with their heads.

Finally the minister with the pointy beard stuttered:

"We totally agree with our king. You all have paid enough for the rest of your lives."

"We were blinded by greed", confirmed the fat minister, with blushing cheeks.

"Yes, yes, that is right", spluttered the minister with the tight collar.

The kobold king slapped his hands on the table enthusiastically and shouted happily:

"That is great news!"

"Wonderful!", the elf called out spontaneously. The owl fluttered his wings in excitement and Pim the squirrel wagged gaily with his tail. The kobold king threw a glance at Pim, the owl and the elf.

"Out of our gratitude we want to invite you, the ministers and the scholars for a feast." The elf nodded heavily. The little bob on his cap swung back and forward as he shouted:

"A party is always fun!" The giant king had to laugh:

"I have heard about your reputation as partygoers. But since we have a whole basin filled with Bubbly Azules Shake we would like to invite you and your entire fellow countrymen for a party here."

The kobold king nodded gaily to the giant king and reacted spontaneously:

"We gladly accept your invitation!" Then the

giant king pointed towards Brave Hunter.

"And you are our guest of honour." Brave Hunter blushed shyly but shook his head and said hesitantly.

"I would love to accept your invitation. But we have to leave as early as possible tomorrow morning. We have lost so much precious time."

Jan, the minister, got up and walked to the giant king, and whispered in his ear. The giant king nodded enthusiastically and mumbled kindly:

"Off course that can be arranged", Jan looked at the group and announced:

"Our biggest and strongest giants will take you and your horses on their backs to the borders of Wizard County. They can bring you there in one day."

"Great idea!" Bram cheered gladly, "that way you can be at the party!"

"Yippee", yelled Neston joyfully. Norma, Lauren and Alice jumped up enthusiastically. All five were dancing around in a circle. Pim looked at the dancing circle and bowed to Brave Hunter.

"Look how joyful everyone is." Brave Hunter nodded and agreed:

"Yes, we could sure use a mirror like that in the human world. But I am afraid that there won't be enough mirrors." Brave Hunter made a face. Pim wagged his tail and reacted wisely:

"I understand what you mean. Humans really make a mess of things and think that they own the world. We animals don't understand that at all. The earth is there for everyone, but humans think that they are the only one's that count on the earth."

Brave Hunter nodded cautiously.

"Indeed, many dumb people are only consumed with their own self interest. But I believe that when you try to be as good and honest as you can, ignorant people can come to their senses. In a way you hold a mirror in front of them."

"What are you both talking about so seriously", said the elf, who had walked towards them cheerfully. He threw an arm around the shoul-ders of Brave Hunter and Pim and said brightly:

"Come on, we have something to celebrate!" Brave Hunter and Pim smiled and said simultaneously:

"We have indeed!"